Accidental Attraction

By Kenadee Bryant

Accidental Attraction

Limitless Publishing, LLC
Kailua, HI 96734
www.limitlesspublishing.com

Formatting: Limitless Publishing

ISBN-13: 978-1-68058-835-4
ISBN-10: 1-680585-835-4

Dedication

Dedicated to my family. Thank you for putting up with my craziness and doing everything for me. I couldn't ask for a better family.

Chapter One

Jenna

You know that feeling you get when you embarrass yourself in front of someone, and you know you have to face them the next day? That dread and nervousness wrapping itself around you like a cocoon? Just the idea of having to face that person again so soon and just wishing you could crawl into a hole and die? Well, I was certainly feeling that way right now. The fact that I had to see Liam today after what happened last night was not appealing in the slightest. I just wanted to crawl back into bed and stay there all day. I hadn't slept again last night, and I was beyond tired. I had gotten so used to not doing anything and sleeping all day that my body was no longer used to being up for hours at a time.

I was currently sitting on the couch, staring blankly at the TV while some kid's show was playing. I was still in my PJs, waiting for Lennon to come over and help me get dressed for my engagement pictures, which were being taken in just a few hours. I couldn't lie and say last night wasn't great. Seeing Liam being all cute and sweet with Sky made made me question how I felt about him. But I knew there was no way I could start liking Liam. I had only known him almost a month, and the whole time he had ignored me and been rude to me.

I was just worried about seeing him later today. Would he bring up what happened? In a way I didn't want him to, and it would just be better if he didn't. I mean, we hadn't even kissed. It was just in the heat of the moment. If Candy hadn't knocked on the door, I didn't know if we would have kissed or if Liam would have stopped it. A part of me had really wanted to kiss him. I mean, who wouldn't? He was gorgeous. On top of me not really wanting to see Liam, we had to take our engagement photos today. I knew his family would be there. Liam and I would have to act all lovey-dovey. It seemed my life had turned into one big soap opera. *Just act normal around him. If he has forgotten about the almost-kiss, then you need to as well.* I could do this. I could take photos with my fake future husband while his family was there and then later take manners classes with Lennon. I sighed and leaned my head on the couch. I was really starting to hate my life.

So here I sat, in my PJs, watching TV but not really paying attention. I had strict orders from Lennon because she wanted to be in charge of everything so the photos would look amazing. Not that I really minded, since I sucked at doing makeup. I had already showered early this morning, so at least that was done. Since I hadn't slept much last night, I got up soon after Liam left, not wanting to face him. It was now eleven, and Lennon should be here any second. Our appointment with the photographer was at one. Apparently that was the perfect time to take pictures outside. I honestly didn't even know where we were taking them, or anything about today, really. All I knew was that we would be taking quite a few pictures, and most of them would be outside. Things were going to go *great* today. Note the sarcasm. The bride-to-be didn't even know what was going on.

There was a knock on the front door before it swung open, revealing Lennon with her arms filled with all different kinds of bags.

"I am here, so let's get this bitch started!" she yelled, slamming the door behind her. I shook my head but chuckled softly under my breath. I turned the television off and stood up, trailing behind her as she walked to my room. I had only known Lennon a few days, but I had already discovered she had a big personality and didn't care what others thought of her. I loved the way she held herself; it was slowly becoming one of my favorite things about her. I noticed, as I followed after her, that she was wearing a cute white summer dress that had birds on it. It fit her slender body perfectly and highlighted her naturally tan skin.

"Okay, we have a lot to do!" she exclaimed, setting stuff on my bed and the vanity off in the corner of my room.

"How much is a lot?" I asked. As she turned

toward me, her eyes widened.

"A lot! Look at the bags under your eyes! Did you even sleep last night?"

"Thanks, that makes me feel amazing," I said sarcastically, taking a seat in front of the mirror.

"You know these photos are going to be seen by hundreds of people, right? We have to make you look amazing." I hadn't really thought about people seeing the photos, and now that she mentioned it, I felt a little more nervous. "Don't worry. I'll work my magic. So first, let's do makeup, then hair, then let's get you dressed." Taking my long blonde hair, she put it in a messy bun at the top of my head before turning me around and starting on my face.

About fifteen minutes later, she let me look in the mirror, and I found a different Jenna staring back at me. The bags under my eyes were gone, my skin looked flawless and glowing, my green eyes stood out against my dark eyelashes and eye shadow, and my lips were a pale pink. I wouldn't go as far to say I looked like a whole different person, but I did look different. The makeup was natural. I didn't look or feel like I had gallons of it caked on my face, thankfully.

"Okay, now your hair," Lennon said, taking my hair out of its bun. My hair was honestly the thing I liked most about myself. It was long and thick, with just a little bit of curl at the ends. "I love your hair."

"Thanks, I grow it myself," I said. Both of us let out a laugh, shaking our heads. "So, you haven't told me what happened last night after I left. Did Liam come home and get mad?" Lennon asked, brushing my hair and looking at me in the mirror's reflection. It was a foreign feeling, having someone brush my hair for me. When my mom left, it was up to me to take care of myself.

"He was already home when I walked in."

"He was? What happened?" I gave her the whole rundown, from when I walked in until when Candy arrived, but I left out the part about Liam and me almost kissing. I wanted that to stay private because I didn't even know how I felt about it yet. "Wow. He is great with kids though, isn't he?" she said.

"You don't sound surprised that he is," I said, looking at her.

"He always has been good with kids. His cousins, Blake's younger sister. There's just something about him that kids like." *And women,* I added silently.

"He had Sky wrapped around his finger. It was cute," I said after staring into the mirror.

"Jenna, he is a good guy. Just give him some time to open up." I nodded, wanting to believe it. I didn't know if Liam would ever become comfortable enough around me to let me in.

"Do you know what we are doing for our engagement photos?" I asked.

"Well, Liam hired the best photographer out there, so it kind of is up to him on what he wants you guys to do. I do know it is going to be something simple, cute yet elegant. I mean, the entire city is going to see it in a few days, so it has to look amazing. Both Liam and you will be wearing something a little formal, but still casual. Don't worry, Jenna, it is going to be fine."

"Who's all going to be there, anyways?"

"Let's see. Me, Blake, Liam's parents, Julie, maybe a friend of his parents', but that should be it," she explained. Okay, not too many. I could deal with that. But I was not sure why they all needed to be there with us. "Your hair is done. Now clothes." Lennon had just curled my hair into soft waves that cascaded down my back, and there were a few pieces framing my face. "I brought a few dresses, since we seem to be close to the same size. If we don't like any of these, we can do something else." She went over to the bag on my bed and unzipped it, pulling out three dresses.

"Okay, so all three are simple yet cute. Here's a white one, a pale peach, and a blue." The white one and peach one were both lace, and the white one had little triangle cuts in the middle. Grabbing that one first, I went to the bathroom and slipped off my PJs and into the dress. Thankfully it had a zipper up the back so I wouldn't ruin my hair. The moment I put it on, I immediately said no. My boobs felt squished in the top, and the bottom was a little too short for something like this. Opening the door a crack, I put my hand out and asked for the peach one and handed Lennon back the white one.

The second I slipped it on, I wanted to wear it. The pale peach color made my arms and legs look tanner than they actually were. It had quarter-length lace sleeves, a lace neckline, and the body was a solid peach color with thin lace over the top, and a thin black belt. It came to my fingertips, making it kind of short, but not slutty short. I managed to zip the back up the entire way and smooth it out, staring in the mirror. My blonde curls looked perfect, as did my makeup. I looked amazing. When I stepped out of the room, Lennon grinned widely at me as I did a twirl for her.

"Perfect, absolutely perfect. That dress was made for you. Here, put these on." She handed me a pair of nude heels to go with the dress. Once I had them on, I felt like the entire outfit came together. "Liam is not going to be able to take his hands off of you today," Lennon said smugly. I rolled my eyes, not bothering to answer. Going over to the vanity, I grabbed my favorite necklace and put it on. The moon-shaped jewel rested right in the middle of my chest, the light blue stone in the middle of the moon shining from the light. This was the only thing my mother had ever given me. I realized that ever since I came to live here, I hadn't worn it. I hadn't even thought about it, actually. I used to wear it every day and night. It always made me feel closer to my mom, like I would always have a piece of her with me. I looked in the mirror and nodded, feeling complete and ready.

"I love that necklace," Lennon said from behind me.

"Thanks. It was from my mom," I said, running my thumb over the pendant.

"It's beautiful. We'd better get going. It will take a little bit to get there." Nodding, I grabbed my phone from the bed and the handbag Lennon had gotten together for me. "Oh wait! Your ring!"

"Thank God you reminded me." Going over to my bedside table, I pulled my ring box out and slipped my engagement ring on my ring finger. I stared down at it, still amazed by how big it was and how weird it felt.

"Ready to go?" Lennon called from the door, making me look up. Nodding, I put the box back and followed after her. While we walked to the front door, my legs wobbled from the heels. I wasn't used such high ones or heels in general. It was going to be a miracle if I didn't fall today.

The car ride didn't take long, and the closer we got the more nervous I became. I played with the hem of my dress, then my ring and necklace. It wasn't that I was nervous to see Liam's family again. It was him I was nervous about. I knew I was overthinking this and I shouldn't be, but I couldn't help it. When Lennon put the car in park, I stared at where we were in surprise. I thought we were going somewhere in the city, but instead we were at Liam's parents' house.

"I didn't know we were taking pictures here."

"This is a great place. There's a huge field, a barn a bit further away. They even have a lake over there," Lennon pointed out when we got out of the car. When I was here last, I hadn't paying attention to anything, apparently. I hadn't noticed they had a lake or a barn! I guess I was too worried about meeting his family. This place was amazing and would be a great place to take our photos.

"Did Liam's parents always live here?" I asked, watching my step as we walked to the door.

"Yes. Well, no. This is their 'summer' home. When we were all younger our families would come here to get away from the city. This is his parents' third home. They have a house closer to the city

8

where Liam grew up, as did we, and then they have one in the Hamptons. His parents come here more often, since they have horses and such. Plus it is close enough to the city that they can take a quick drive there if they need," Lennon explained.

Lennon didn't even bother to knock on the door. She just walked right in, yelling that we'd arrived. Shutting the door behind me and looking around the foyer, I was struck again by how simply yet unique the house was decorated, and the size of it. It was a cabin mixed with a house. The moment you stepped through the door, the house automatically had a homey feeling. After I finished gawking, I noticed Lennon had walked away. I followed the voices to the large living room located at the back of the house.

"There you are, Jenna," Lilly, Liam's mother, said the moment I came into view. She stood up in a second flat and gave me a tight hug. Awkwardly, I hugged her back, still not used to being hugged.

"Hi, Lilly," I greeted once she pulled away from me. Looking around the room, I saw Liam's father, Adam, in one chair, Julie, Liam's sister, on the couch sitting next to Lennon, and an older man I didn't recognize sitting across from Adam.

"Jenna, it's great to see you again," Adam said, smiling and standing up to hug me as well. "Brian, this is Jenna Howard, Liam's fiancé. Jenna, this is Brian Mathews. He's a family friend and colleague," he said, introducing the man across from him. Standing up, Brian made his way toward me. He was tall, not as tall as Liam though, and looked to be a little older than Adam. The color of

9

his hair had turned salt-and-pepper, but he had a pair of brown eyes that still seemed to sparkle. He had laugh lines around them and a kind smile that made me like him almost instantly.

"Hello, Jenna, it's nice to meet you," he greeted me. Instead of hugging me like Liam's parents, he grabbed my hand and brought it to his lips, placing a soft kiss on it. I blushed, looking over at Julie and Lennon only to find them rolling their eyes and smiling at us. "Liam didn't say his fiancé was such a beauty," he said, pulling away but grinning at me. My blush deepened. I opened my mouth to say something but was cut off by a deep voice behind me.

"Old man, she is too young for you." Turning around, I saw Blake walking into the room, shaking his head at Brian.

"Who are you calling old, young man?" Brian asked, but he didn't sound remotely offended.

"You, you're like eighty years old and hitting on a young girl who is engaged to another man," Blake shot back, sending me a grin before hugging Lilly and shaking Adam's hand. For a second, I was scared that he had made Brian mad, but a deep chuckle from beside me told me he wasn't.

"What can I say? I like them young, kid."

I put a hand over my mouth to stop my laugh from escaping. I looked between Blake and Brian, wondering why they were talking that way to each other.

"Brian is Blake's uncle," Lilly said, likely seeing the confusion on my face. "Don't listen to them. They do this all the time, making jabs at one another." She waved her hand at them.

"Where's Liam?" Julie asked from over on the couch.

"His phone rang right after we pulled up, but he should be in in a second," Blake replied. I watched as he made his way to the couch Lennon and Julie were occupying. It was a medium-sized couch, but with two people already on it I knew Blake's big frame wouldn't fit. That didn't stop him, of course. He squeezed in next to Lennon, who in turn tried to push him off, but I could see she actually liked that he sat next to her when there was a lot of empty seats. When I looked at them, I knew they would make a great couple.

"Liam, you never told me your fiancé was very pleasing to the eye," Brian said, making me turn my gaze away from Lennon and Blake toward the doorway of the living room. Liam walked in, and I felt my mouth go dry. He looked absolutely scrumptious. He was dressed in a pair of black dress pants and a white button-up dress shirt that had the sleeves rolled up to the elbows and a few buttons done at the top. His brown hair was in its signature messy but sexy look. His outfit was so simple, yet he pulled it off like he had just walked out of a magazine or runway. He didn't even look like he had just come from work.

Why was I suddenly noticing how nice-looking Liam was? Maybe last night opened my eyes, because seeing him there with an easy smile on his face, with his hands tucked into his pockets, made me want to jump him and kiss him all over. My lack of sleep was starting to get to me. Before yesterday

I hadn't even wanted anything to do with Liam, and now today I wanted to run my tongue down his chest. *Woah, where did that thought come from?* I was surprised at myself. There was something seriously going on with me.

"I didn't say anything because I didn't want your old ass to steal her," I heard Liam's velvety voice say, interrupting my scandalous thoughts. "Hey, babe," he said, coming to a stop beside me. He wrapped an arm around my waist and laid a quick, gentle kiss to my temple before greeting his family. *Jenna, just remember this is all an act. He is only doing this so his parents believe us,* I repeated to myself when I felt my stomach do somersaults at the kiss. I looked up at him, almost waiting for him to act different from last night, but he looked fine, relaxed and happy even.

"Well, in that dress anyone would want to," I heard Brian say, tuning back into the conversation.

"You are right about that," Liam muttered, looking me up and down. Gulping, I stared back at him, wanting more than anything to be able to hear his thoughts right now. "Where is Leonardo?" he said more loudly a second later, looking away from me.

"He should be here in a second," Lilly answered. Not even a second later, there was a knock on the door, and Lilly went to go answer it. Glancing around at everyone, I wondered why they were here honestly; it wasn't like we were taking pictures with them. I did notice Adam, Brian, and Blake were dressed casual in jeans and a t-shirt or collared shirt. Julie, Lennon, and Lilly were wearing dresses.

"Okay, everybody, listen up!" I heard a new, Italian-accented voice shout suddenly. I jumped into Liam and turned toward the voice. Walking in was a very attractive guy with shoulder-length black hair, wearing ripped jeans and a t-shirt. His face was gorgeous, and when he looked over at Liam, I saw he had grey eyes. *Wow, he is cute.* In his arms was what looked like a camera stool and a big camera hanging from his neck.

"This will only take an hour. I want the bride and the groom to follow me outside. We will be doing different poses in different places, and you may have to change your clothes, sir, but the bride won't. After getting some with you, we will get the bridesmaids and groomsmen with you," he said all at once. I stood there shocked, trying to take it all in. When we didn't immediately follow him, he snapped his fingers and jerked his head at us. Liam and I quickly followed after him.

"He's a little scary," I whispered to Liam as we made our way out the back door and down the steps, leading to a big empty field.

"Yeah, but he is the best in the business," he replied, grabbing my hand as I wobbled on my heels. Sending him a grateful smile, I walked beside him, liking the feeling of his hand in mine. It seemed like our hands were made for each other, because his big one fit perfectly with my small one.

"Sir and my lady, stand here," Leonardo said, gesturing at the patch of long grass in the field. I found it weird he was calling me "my lady," but his sexy Italian accent made me forget about it. "Bride, stand in front of him. Groom, wrap your arms around her waist and pull her back toward you," he instructed.

"Just call us Liam and Jenna," I said, getting into my position. Leonardo acted like I didn't even speak and continued on shouting at Liam to get behind me.

"God damn," Liam muttered in my ear as he stood behind me, bringing his arms around my waist. I let out a giggle but swallowed it as Leonardo shot me a hard glance.

"Bride, bring your arms up and wrap around his neck." The position felt awkward. "Now smile." He brought his camera up to his face and started clicking away, even though Liam and I weren't ready.

For the next fifteen minutes, Leonardo shouted at Liam and me to get into different poses. It was kind of awkward as we wrapped our arms around another and pressed in each other's bodies. Every time one of us moved too slowly for him, he would yell at us and Liam would mutter curses under his breath. We were now over by a wooden fence, and I was being instructed to sit on top of the fence while Liam stood between my legs.

"Does he realize I am wearing a dress and heels?" I asked Liam as I tried to climb on top of the fence. "Because I don't think he does." After I failed at getting on Liam, he just chuckled and grabbed me by the waist and hoisted me up and onto the top of the fence. I stared at him, wide-eyed. "Well, that is one way to do it," I commented.

"Well, I was getting tired of seeing your underwear," Liam said, smirking as he spread my legs a little and stepped in between them.

"Hey!" I exclaimed, actually getting worried that I had flashed him. He just laughed at my expression and leaned a little into me. Even though I was high up, he still towered over me, making me look up at him.

"Don't worry. I don't mind grandma undies," he whispered, leaning his head down. I stared up at him with my mouth wide open, trying to come up with a good comeback.

"They are not grandma undies," I hissed, not caring it wasn't really a comeback.

"It's okay, babe. I don't mind." I went to hit him, but he took a step back and grinned at me.

"Groom, now go on the other side. Bride, get down," Leo ordered. Rolling my eyes at him, I carefully slid down the fence so I wouldn't fall and twist my ankle in my heels. In one quick motion, Liam had grabbed the fence and jumped over it.

"Showoff," I muttered but listened to Leo ordering us into another pose. "For your information, my panties are very cute, and you won't be seeing them," I said and leaned with my hands in front of me on the fence while Liam did the same thing.

"Oh, Jenna, who says I won't be seeing them?" He smirked at me.

"Me," I shot back at him with a smirk, moving closer and bringing my leg up in order to do so. Our faces were inches apart, and I could make out little silver sparks in Liam's eyes I hadn't noticed before. Being this close to Liam, I forgot about Leonardo snapping photos of us and shouting things at us.

"Don't worry, your panties are very cute," he whispered before moving back once again. I stared back at him, not really knowing what to say or do. "Come on, honeybunch, Leonardo wants us to go somewhere else." His voice all sweet, but he had a stupid smirk on his face. I glared at him, pushing off the fence and following behind him.

"Groom, I want you here, and I want you to pick up the bride," Leo said. Both Liam and I had told him to call us by our names, but he still didn't listen. "Bride, when he picks you up by the waist, lean down and kiss him. Maybe put your leg up," he said, moving backwards to get a good angle. I stood there wondering if I heard him right, that I would have to kiss Liam.

"Pumpkin, come on," Liam said from behind me. Over the last half an hour, he had probably called me every single romantic term.

"You better not drop me, Liam, or I swear to God I will kill you," I warned, pointing at him as I made my way to him.

"I promise I won't…unless you weigh a lot." I smacked his arm, then put my hands on his shoulder and took a deep breath. *Please don't drop me,* I chanted silently as Liam put his hands on my waist. He softly counted to three before lifting me up effortlessly. My face was an inch away from his, and his minty breath fanned against me. His lips looked so soft and inviting as he stared up at me. My hair tumbled down around us, almost like a shield. Maybe it was being this close to him, but the need to kiss him came back in full force. I looked at his face, almost memorizing it as he kept me suspended in the air. My hold on his shoulders loosened, and my fingers slowly made their way up his neck and the side of his jaw. The muscle jumped beneath my fingers as I made my way to his cheeks. My breath was coming out in pants, and my teeth came out to bite my bottom lip. The longer I stared down at Liam, the more I wanted to feel his lips against mine.

Everything and everyone around us faded in the background. All there was was Liam staring up at me, his blue eyes darkening. His lips parted, and he somehow brought his face closer to mine. The moment I felt his lips graze mine, I threw everything out of my mind and brought my lips down, capturing his. My hands cupped his cheeks while he held me up, but I felt the slightest touch of his fingers or thumb rubbing my waist. The kiss lasted longer than a second. Instead, we sunk into it.

His lips became almost demanding as he moved them against mine. I kissed him back hard and let out a small moan as I felt his tongue slip out and trace my lips, almost asking me permission for entry. Giving it, I parted my lips. My hands moved up into his hair, and I gripped it between my fingers. All I could think about at the moment was his lips and mine. Nothing else mattered. I was slightly aware that my leg was starting to rise. For a split second, I thought of *The Princess Diaries* and the whole foot-popping thing, but it was gone in an instant as Liam's tongue circled mine.

I felt Liam's arms bringing me down, but we didn't break away. Instead, he wrapped his arms tight around my waist, crushing me into his chest, my toes barely touching the ground. Gripping his hair, I twirled my tongue with his. I didn't care that I needed oxygen at the moment. Liam was my oxygen. I don't know how long we kissed, but we finally broke away and panted staring at each other. My lips felt swollen, and when I looked at Liam I saw his were too. With our arms still wrapped around one another, I wanted to smile. I had given my first kiss to Liam, and in that moment, I didn't regret it at all.

Chapter Two

I had given my first kiss to Liam, and in that moment, I didn't regret it at all.

I stared at Liam after we pulled away from the kiss. My lips were tingling and felt swollen. In fact, my whole body felt like it was tingling, and my knees were threatening to give out. Since that was my first kiss, I had nothing to compare it to, but I knew Liam was experienced, and with the way he was acting, it had to be good. Right? He was staring down at me almost in shock or even surprise.

The longer he stood there staring at me in silence, the worry that the kiss wasn't good or that he would turn away from me was starting to grow. I was still pressed tight against him, my heart beating hard in my chest. Automatically I moved my head back, waiting for Liam to blow up and start yelling at me.

"Okay, enough smoochy-smoochy. Time to take pictures with the rest of the wedding party," Leonardo said, interrupting our staring contest.

19

With Liam's silence dragging out even more, I felt my heart start to sink. He thought the kiss was a mistake. He would probably yell at me the moment we got home so his parents didn't think anything was wrong between us. Pushing back the tears that wanted to fall, I swallowed the lump in my throat. It was stupid of me to think Liam would like or want to kiss me. I was so repulsive that the moment after I kissed him, he regretted it. Just as I was starting to move out of Liam's strong hold, he surprised me by planting a small kiss on my lips again before unwrapping his arms from my waist.

I stood there shocked, trying to process the fact Liam just *voluntarily* kissed me, again. He wasn't running away or yelling at me. In fact, he was looking down at me with a small smile on his face. As he held his hand out, I slid mine inside it, swallowing the shock I was feeling. I needed to relish the fact that he was acting normal around me. I trailed alongside him as we walked back to the house, our silence actually comfortable. The moment we stepped into the house everyone stood up, and Lennon shot me a wide grin like she knew what just happened. Next to her Blake smiled, winking at Liam and me.

"Liam, go and put this on under your dress shirt," Blake said, throwing something blue toward Liam, who caught it one-handed. He nodded like he knew what it was before sending me a small smile and dropping my hand, heading to the bathroom to change. I stared after him, my emotions going everywhere. Maybe this was what Lennon was talking about, how Liam was great once you got to know him.

"Bridesmaids and groomsmen, come here," Leonardo yelled, even though we were all right there. I looked over at the photographer, but my attention was drawn to the new arrival. He was cute. Very cute, actually. As he stood next to Blake, I could see he was the same height, maybe an inch shorter, with short, light brown hair. I could only see half of his face, but from here I could see a great jaw line. There was something hot about a man's jaw line. He was dressed like Liam and Blake, with a white dress shirt that showed off his well-built arms, and he also wore black dress pants. I stood there wondering who he was and why he was here, not hearing anything Leonardo was saying. I felt a soft nudge on my arm, so I pulled my eyes away from the new guy and saw Liam standing next to me, looking the same as he did before.

"Ready to go?" he asked.

"Uh, what?" I asked, confused.

"You didn't hear a word he said, did you?" Liam asked, a grin spreading across his face.

"No, of course I did. I just didn't hear you," I lied, lifting my chin up and folding my arms across my chest. I turned to face him.

"Uh-huh." He looked at me with a smirk. He obviously knew I was lying. "Then where are we going?" He took a step closer to me. His close proximity to me made my mouth dry and my mind blank for a minute. "Jenna," he taunted.

"We are going outside," I said. "Come on, we don't want to be late." I smirked at him, grabbing his hand and pulling him behind me out the door to the backyard.

"There you are. Would you two stop making out so we can get this done?" Blake yelled at us the moment we stepped outside. I blushed but continued pulling Liam with me.

"Jenna, you are more than welcome to walk with me instead of Liam," Brian called from ahead of us. I let out a laugh as Liam, Blake, and the new guy immediately started yelling back at him about him being too old and to find his own girl. It might seem weird that a guy that could be my grandpa's age was flirting with me, but it really wasn't. It was who he was, and besides, it was friendly flirting, not I-want-you-now flirting.

"So who is the new guy?" I whispered to Liam as we followed Leonardo.

"That is Grayson Patterson. He's a friend from college and works at the company with me," Liam answered.

All of us, Liam's parents and Brian included, walked through the backyard for a few minutes before we finally came to a stop in front of a gorgeous lake. It wasn't huge, but it was big enough for canoes, and it would be a workout swimming from one side to the other. Trees lined the edge of the water, making it almost secluded and shady. There was a deck that led a little ways onto the lake. Taking pictures here was definitely a good idea.

"Okay, first, let's do a couple with the bride and groom, then with the rest of you," Leo said, interrupting my staring. Pushing aside the awkward feeling of having everyone watch Liam and me pose for pictures, I let Liam pull me to where Leo wanted us. "I want you guys to hold hands between your bodies and lean in toward one another. Go." When I rolled my eyes, I earned a chuckle from Liam as we did as we were told. I couldn't help but feel like Liam and I were pieces of clay being moved and sculpted the way Leo wanted.

"Why did you pick him?" I muttered to Liam, leaning my face toward his.

"Well, you know he is hot. He's kind of my type. Didn't you know?" he answered, grinning at me. I couldn't help but grin and laugh. I wanted to shake my head at him, but with Leonardo yelling at us to stay exactly like that, I didn't.

"I didn't know you fancied men, especially Italian men." I grinned at him.

"Don't you know the accent is one of the reasons he's my side babe?" He wiggled his eyebrows at me, and I let out a loud laugh.

"Good, now turn around with your backs to one another. Bride, make a face while you, groom, smirk." With Liam's lower back pressed to mine, I crossed my arms over my chest and scrunched up my face. I could practically feel Liam wearing a giant smirk. We only spent a few more minutes posing before Leonardo gestured for the rest of the group to come over. Having not paid attention all afternoon, I suddenly realized Julie and Lennon were my bridesmaids, while Blake and Grayson were Liam's groomsmen. I felt sad that I didn't have a say in who my bridesmaids were, but at least I had two great, nice girls. Besides, I didn't want to drag Sophia or Candy into my mess of a life more than I had to.

"So we are trying the pose that one of the bridesmaids thought of?" Leonardo asked, and I glanced over at Liam's sister and Lennon, confused.

"Yes." Lennon nodded, then turned to me. "You are going to love this idea. I gave each of the boys a superhero t-shirt to wear under their shirts, so while we stand next to them, they will open their shirts and like they are ripping their shirts with it underneath. I saw it on Pinterest and knew we had to do it," she explained. I liked the idea, and I was about to say yes when the voices of the boys echoed around us.

"Dude, I still don't get why I had to be Iron Man. Why couldn't I be Batman?" Grayson asked, almost whining. All three guys were unbuttoning the tops of their shirts, showing what superhero shirt they got.

"Because I am cooler than you," Blake said with a smirk.

"Nobody is cooler than Superman, dip-weeds," Liam shot in. The three of them were acting like kids, arguing who was the better hero.

"I can't believe you like that one," I said playfully to Lennon, nodding to Blake, who was currently putting Grayson in a headlock.

"Well, you are marrying that one," Lennon replied, pointing at Liam, who was standing there staring at the two grown men about to wrestle. He seemed to be saying something to them under his breath, but I knew it was nothing to get them to stop.

"Sadly, you are right."

"Both of your men are such dorks," Julie butted

in, shaking her head at them.

"Hey, yours is currently getting manhandled by Blake," Lennon pointed out.

"Wait, you like Grayson?" I asked, turning to her. I could actually see the two of them as a cute couple. Plus, it would make sense for her to like one of Liam's friends, same with Lennon.

"No, it's not a big deal. I just think he's hot," Julie said, but from the way she was looking over at Grayson, I knew it wasn't just a crush. She felt something deeper for him. Next to me, Lennon rolled her eyes.

"We better break them up before they ruin their clothes," I commented, to which they both nodded. "Hey, guys, stop!" I yelled, but I wasn't heard over Lennon, who marched right up to all three and hollered.

"Hey, dickheads, cut it out. We want to finish this!" She was practically yelling in Blake and Grayson's ears, making them stop and pull away from one another. "Good boys." She stood on her toes to pat their heads like dogs. I grinned at her, shaking my head slightly before going to stand by Liam. While all this was going down, Lilly, Adam, and Brian were sitting on a bench in the shade, talking quietly and looking over at us every once in a while. Don't even ask me why they were even here.

"Everyone!" Leo raised his voice at us. "Only a few more pictures. The first one, let's try all the bridesmaids standing a little in front of groomsmen but to the side, holding the shirt like you are ripping it open, revealing the hero shirts underneath. While you are doing that, look at the camera. You can smile if you want, but men look down at your shirts." We all nodded before going to our respective men. Of course it was no surprise Lennon was with Blake, and Julie with Grayson.

"Make sure not to really rip my shirt because you want to see my body," Liam whispered down at me as I gripped the top of his shirt open.

"Please, like I'd like to see your saggy man breasts," I said, smiling sweetly back at him before turning toward the camera. I kept my face straight, staring into the camera as Liam kept his head down, like he was told. The way he was acting with me today caught me so off guard, but I liked it when he was so carefree and funny. He was actually being nice to me and making sarcastic comments. If he would act like this the rest of the time, there would be no trouble with our deal. But a small part of me wanted him to stay cold and mean, because I knew if he continued to act like this around me, I would have no trouble in falling for him. That was something I couldn't do.

"Great! Now, bridesmaids, you guys come over here, and groomsmen, hold your own shirts open and look down at them. Bride and groom, I want you to look at the camera while the bride holds open the shirt, and, groom, hands in your pockets. I want your faces straight," Leo instructed. We were all in position when Leonardo yelled "No!" at Blake and Grayson, making them move closer to us. After a few tries he must have been satisfied with it and stopped.

For the next ten minutes, Leonardo had me with

just my bridesmaids and Liam with just his groomsmen. I didn't know how many pictures we had taken, but my mouth was starting to hurt from smiling, and my feet from my heels. Everyone around us was starting to become antsy and tired, so when Leonardo finally exclaimed that he was done, we all breathed a sigh of relief. As I trudged back to the house, my stomach growled and my throat was dry.

The moment we were back inside the cool house, Liam's mom went to the kitchen to make some lemonade and a few snacks. I offered to help, but of course it was all turned down. Liam and his father led Leonardo to the door and thanked him while he said the pictures would be done by tomorrow if we wanted to come by and pick them out. As soon as the door closed behind him, Blake let out a huge, "Thank God." Leonardo was definitely different than anyone I had ever met.

We all sat in the living room, gabbing together for the next few hours. I learned more about Grayson, that he was Liam and Blake's old college roommate and that he worked in the IT department of Liam's work, making sure things were going well at all the hotels they owned. I watched as Lennon and Blake argued back and forth about stupid things but never getting really mad at each other. I could tell Blake liked her but wasn't going to admit it anytime soon. Same went with Grayson and Julie. Grayson seemed oblivious to Julie flirting with him or her side glances. I talked with Brian some more, feeling so relaxed around him even though he flirted with me more half the time. For a man his age, he was definitely smooth with the ladies.

The whole time I spent at Liam's family home, I laughed and smiled more than I ever had in my life. I felt at home with them, and with all the loud conversations happening around me, I never felt more a part of something. There was something about all these people that made me drop the barriers I had built around myself after my mother left me. For the first time in a long time, I was letting go and allowing myself to be happy. I knew that in a year's time, Liam's parents and sister would probably hate me, because none of this was real and I lied to their faces. I knew that after this year I would go back to being someone with no family and no money, but I didn't care about that at the moment. I ignored the fact that Liam would probably be back to himself later, telling me our kiss was a mistake, and relished in the way he was acting now and how I wanted to kiss him again. I pushed it all to the back of my mind and enjoyed every second of finally feeling like I was part of a family.

***

Liam

If you told me two days ago that I would want to kiss Jenna, I would have laughed in your face. But now, sitting in my parents' living room after having an amazing day, all I wanted to do was grab her and kiss her, despite everyone in the room. Watching her laugh with my friends and family, looking so carefree, made my heart almost ache. Everyone seemed to love her, Brian more than anyone, and seeing the way she acted with them made me want her even more.

She was a totally different girl than I first thought when I found her. I'd originally thought she was some stuck up daddy's girl who was working at a strip club just to piss her dad off. But no, she wasn't that at all. She worked two awful jobs just so she could pay her bills, she had no parents, and her mother fucking abandoned her. The moment I brought her into my house, I wanted to end the deal because I didn't want to deal with her. But after her talking back to me on more than one occasion, and seeing her with Sky last night, something inside of me shifted. Instead of wanting to push her away, I wanted to get to know her. I wanted to know what made her tick: what she liked, what she didn't, what her childhood was like, any future dreams. Just the thought of that scared me, actually. Liam Stanford falling for a girl was unheard of. But something about Jenna made me want to know more about her.

When I had walked through the door earlier, I had a plan for what I was going to do today, but all that went out the window the moment I saw her standing there, in a beautiful simple dress that hugged her body. Her skin looked tan, and her blonde hair was in curls down her back. The dress was simple, but she made it look better almost like she walked out of a magazine. Seeing her standing there, almost comfortable, I could tell she didn't know she was beautiful. She was oblivious to how she looked. Hell, if it hadn't been for that kid Garrett telling our secret, I would have fired him anyways for how he had been staring at Jenna. The way he looked at her body that night made me want to punch his face so he couldn't look at her again. At least I had no worries around Blake, since he was too in love with Lennon to notice anyone else, and Grayson knew she was off limits.

After seeing her looking almost vulnerable this afternoon, I made an unconscious decision to try and act different around her. I was going to use today as the start. While that stupid Italian photographer took our pictures, I couldn't help but like the feel of Jenna's body pressed against mine. She was so little against my big frame, but she somehow fit perfectly against me. I was silently yelling at Leonardo to put us in a pose to kiss. Last night's almost-kiss had run through my mind all night. I regretted the decision to go to my room after helping with Sky and not stay around. I wanted nothing more than Jenna's soft-looking lips on mine.

She had been so close to me last night, and the look in her green eyes as she stared at me had me wanting to press my lips against hers. I would have if there hadn't been a knock on the door. The moment she pulled away, I became aware of all the naughty thoughts running through my mind. I couldn't help but think of her lying beneath me as I kissed along her neck. There was something so enticing to Jenna that made me want her more than any other woman I have ever wanted.

As Jenna's face was an inch from mine, I stared

into her green eyes, watching as it seemed she was having an internal battle. If she hadn't kissed me, I would have kissed her, honestly. The moment her lips met mine, everything about not falling for her disappeared. Her lips were just as soft as I thought, and her soft little moan was hotter than anything I had ever heard. I didn't want the kiss to stop, and when it did, I had to catch my breath. She stared at me with doe eyes, making me feel like putty in her hands. I barely heard what Leonardo was saying, and clearly Jenna wasn't listening either. Surprising both her and me, I laid a soft kiss to her lips before grabbing her hand and taking her inside.

The rest of the afternoon I kept the need to kiss her at bay, but it was hard as she was pressed against me during the photos. And now, seeing her laughing with my family, the need was stronger. Jenna was making me feel things I hadn't felt in years, and what scared me was that I liked it. I liked how she talked back to me, how she did the opposite of what I instructed her to do. *Jenna Howard, what are you doing to me?*

Chapter Three

Jenna

It was the day after our engagement photos, and I was currently sitting at the kitchen table with Lennon next to me telling me which fork was used for what. I tried to listen, I really did, but my thoughts kept drifting back to Liam. Everything that happened yesterday threw me for a loop, and I didn't know what to think about him. After we all sat around his parents' place for a while, I kept catching him staring at me with a weird expression across his face. Of course seeing him staring at me, I would sneak glances in his direction as well.

It was four o'clock by the time we left his parents'. Liam didn't let me drive with anyone else but him. He was being weird the entire ride home and made the effort to talk to me about the photos and random stuff. I didn't want to ask him why he was acting weird in case it made him stop. When we got home, he got to work making dinner for the both of us.

The rest of the night he talked about everything and anything. I could tell he was trying to act nicer around me and make me feel comfortable. I didn't know what had changed with him, but I wasn't complaining. It was nice being around him and actually having a nice conversation. It was the first time in three weeks that I felt at home and actually wanted by Liam. Whatever was going on, I didn't want it to stop. When we went to bed, he even walked me to my door and said an awkward, "Goodnight."

I had spent a good portion of the night going over everything with a wide grin plastered on my face. I didn't know what time it was when I finally fell asleep, but I knew I still had a smile on my face and an image of Liam's face in my mind. I knew everything wouldn't be suddenly fine and dandy with him when I got up, but when I did I felt lighter than I had before. Maybe it was knowing that Liam was actually being nicer than before.

I missed Liam this morning when he went to work, but it wasn't even an hour later when Lennon showed up, ready to teach me how to act "proper". It still made me angry that I had to do this, but if both Lennon and Liam thought it would help, I'd do it. I was not looking forward to his work party, which was happening in two days. The idea of having to dress up and meet a bunch of new people who thought Liam and I were really getting married was enough to make me throw up in my mouth a little. I didn't like big crowds or attention. I'd rather hide away in the background and let others take the spotlight. Besides raising money, which was the real reason for the Benefit, I knew people were going to be on Liam and me like hounds, asking about our engagement. This afternoon we were supposed to go and pick out a few photos from the shoot, then give them to the paper to print for tomorrow. Tomorrow morning my whole life would change once again. I would be known as the fiancé to one of the richest, most eligible bachelors—Liam Stanford.

"Jenna, are you even listening to me?" Lennon's voice broke through my thoughts.

"Yes, of course."

"Okay, then what is this fork used for?" She held up a smaller fork, but it still looked the same as the other one.

"Salad?" I asked.

"That was an easy one," she said but nodded that I got it right.

"Can we take a break and get something to eat?" I asked, leaning back in my chair. We had been doing this for over two hours, and my brain was fried.

"Fine, but only for a few minutes. We still have a lot to go over." Lennon sighed.

"There's more?" I groaned. "I feel like I'm back in high school." She just shook her head at me.

"I'd make a great teacher."

"Yeah, great at torturing children!" I stood up, heading to the fridge to grab something to eat. "Are you hungry? I can make us something."

"Sure, I'm fine with anything." I spotted some sliced turkey in the fridge and pulled it out. "So, you and Liam kissed, huh?" Lennon said a few minutes later, making me stop putting turkey on our sandwiches.

"It was only a peck on the lips," I said, trying to make it sound like it wasn't a big deal.

"That was not just a peck! It was full-blown making out!" she said. I looked up, finding her leaning against the bar in front of me with a smirk on her face.

"And how would you know?"

"We were all spying, duh, but that doesn't matter." She waved her hand. "You guys looked to be enjoying it."

"Lennon! That's your best friend," I said. I felt a little awkward talking about Liam and me kissing.

"Like I haven't heard about everything from past girlfriends. Seriously though, after that kiss Liam couldn't take his eyes off of you."

"Really?"

"Yes. The whole time we took photos, he was watching you. Same with afterwards, when we were all sitting around the living room."

"I probably had something on my face," I said, finishing up our food and handing her a plate before going back to the table. I wanted what Lennon said to be true, but it was Liam. He wouldn't find me at all attractive.

"And you are just as guilty. You kept glancing at him every chance you got."

"I did not!"

"You so did. Just watching you guys, I can feel the sexual tension," she said. I choked on my sandwich and reached for my water. I felt Lennon's hand softly hitting my back.

"T-There's no sexual tension between us," I choked out.

"You can deny it, but it is there. You guys just need to give in." She sighed and bit into her food.

"You're one to talk! You and Blake couldn't keep your eyes off one another yesterday."

"Now that is a lie. Blake never has and never will see me as more than a friend. I'll always be the brace-faced, nerdy girl from high school," she said in a dejected tone.

"Yeah, right. He literally could not keep his eyes off of you. He purposefully sat beside you when there were plenty of empty seats, and you were the bridesmaid to his groomsman. I know for a fact that if you were Grayson's, he would have thrown a fit. Lenn, honestly, there is no way in hell he does not like you. You are beyond gorgeous, funny, smart, nice."

"Then why hasn't he said something or made any moves to do so? He didn't care when I had a boyfriend a few months ago."

"Maybe he is scared of ruining your friendship, or he just doesn't have the balls to say something. I bet he cared more than he let on about your ex. You may just have to be the one to ask him out. There's no shame in doing that."

"Have you done it before?" she asked, looking at me almost hopefully.

"I, um, I haven't." I cleared my throat and looked down at my plate.

"Jenna, you've had a boyfriend before, right?" Lennon asked. I could feel her gaze on me, but I kept looking down. I felt embarrassed saying I hadn't. She took my silence as my answer. "That can't be true. You're beautiful."

"I just hung in the background during high school. And no one wants to date a girl who doesn't have parents," I said, shrugging. Admitting it out loud didn't hurt anymore. "But let's not talk about that. We should probably finish this before Liam gets home. We have to go and pick out pictures for the papers later," I changed the subject quickly, not wanting the attention.

"Don't think I will let this go so easily, missy." Lennon pointed at me. Grabbing our plates, she put them in the sink and grabbed a huge binder before coming back to the table.

"What is that?" I asked, staring at the binder that was three times thicker than my wrist.

"This is everyone that you will most likely be seeing on Friday. Employees from Stanford Industries will be there, as well as beneficiaries from the company. There will also be some of the top A-listers from New York companies. We need you to be familiar with all of them so when they come up to you at the Benefit, you will be able to talk to them. Let's get started." She rubbed her hands together and opened the binder. I groaned, already dreading the next hour or so.

***

"Lennon, if you so much as say another person's name I will kill you," I threatened exactly two hours later. My brain was beyond fried, and my head was pounding. It was now one, and I was more than

37

ready to be done. Lennon was a torturous teacher. On more than one occasion, I'd wanted to strangle her.

"Jenna, one more. Who is Martin Brotherson?" she asked.

"He is Vice President and Founder of Brotherson's Inc. They sell everything from furniture to electronic items. He has brown hair, which he probably has to dye. He is in his late forties. His wife is Karen Brotherson, and he has a daughter named Tessa and a son named Ryan; they are twins and thirteen years old. I think they are at some boarding school," I mumbled into my arms, where I rested my head. "There. Can we be done now?"

"Wow, I'm impressed you learned everyone's name and things about them. I was expecting to come over tomorrow and finish up, but now I don't have to."

"Thank the Lord," I mumbled.

"Why aren't you in school? You're really smart."

"I never had the money to go. I couldn't even make it to high school most of the time, so why spend the money for college to have the same problem?" I shrugged, getting up to get a drink.

"Maybe now you can! You could take a few classes," Lennon said, following me.

"I don't know." I'd never thought about going to college. It was always something that I couldn't do. I mean, I did okay in high school. I would have done better if I knew I could get in somewhere or if I had a future. I wasn't stupid. In fact, I was pretty smart, but the whole idea of going to college was foreign to me.

"Just think about it, it couldn't hurt to look into it. I'd better get going. A girl that I do makeup for needs me for something. I'll text you later. Have fun with Liam." She winked at me before pulling me into a hug and leaving.

Exiting the kitchen, I headed up to the library to do some reading before Liam got home. I hadn't read in a while, and I was starting to have withdrawals. I'd finished *1984*, so I searched the rows of books for something to catch my eye. As I browsed around, a familiar black cover caught the corner of my eye. Pulling it out, I let out a laugh when I saw the title. Never in a million years did I think Liam would read or have *Twilight*. I shook my head, laughing softly as I noticed he had the entire series. With the book still in my hand, I headed for the comfortable chair in the corner. I'd never read it before, but I'd heard it was good. Tucking my fuzzy-socked feet under me, I dove into the story.

I didn't know how long I was reading for, but when I finally looked up, Liam was standing in the doorway watching me. I blushed, realizing that he had called my name a few times but I hadn't answered. I was so engrossed in the book I didn't realize he was home already. I was a good ninety pages into it, and I could see why it was such a big hit. The author did a great job at pulling the reader into this world where vampires and werewolves existed.

"Uh, sorry, I didn't hear you," I said quietly, almost like I would wake the books up. There was something about being in any library that made you whisper.

"What are you reading?" Liam asked, his deep voice loud to my ear after hours of silence. At the mention of *Twilight,* I grinned, walking toward him with it pressed to my chest so he wouldn't see what it was.

"I didn't know you read the entire series of *Twilight.*" I couldn't keep myself from mocking him.

"What? I've never read those," he defended himself, but I could tell he was lying by the little bit of pink in his cheeks.

"So they are just here for no reason?" I should have just dropped it, but it was fun teasing Liam. It didn't happen every day.

"It is just there to fill up space."

"Riiiiight. We need re-vamp your books in here. They are all older ones," I said, dropping the *Twilight* comments, but I couldn't wipe the grin off my face.

"You're probably right. I haven't read half of these," he said as he looked around the room. "How about we go to a bookstore after we drop off the photos?"

"Sounds good to me." I smiled at him. Even if he didn't realize the simple gesture to get me more books was sweet, I did.

"Ready to go?"

"Yeah, just let me change and get some shoes on." Brushing by him, I ignored the tingling feel that spread across my arm when it touched his. I walked quickly to my room and slipped off my PJ bottoms and threw on my trusty pair of blue jeans. Sliding on my Converse, I grabbed my ring before I forgot it, then grabbed my bag and headed to find Liam so we could leave. It was probably a good idea to wear my engagement ring when we dropped off the photos.

I found Liam standing by the garage waiting patiently with me. Sending me a heart-stopping smile, he gestured for me to lead the way. As I walked to the garage, I realized that was only the second time Liam had ever really smiled at me. He usually just smirked or kept his lips in a thin line. I was already liking this new side to him.

I slid in the passenger seat of the Jeep, and Liam backed out and started to drive to wherever we were going. When I turned the radio up, I nodded along to "Shut Up And Dance." The ride to pick up the photos was quick. Turning the car off, Liam jumped out and ran to my door before I could open it myself. He held out his hand for me, and I blushed and smiled, putting mine inside of his. Following beside, we walked inside a huge, nice-looking building. A bell chimed above us as we entered, and I immediately heard the voice of Leonardo yelling at us.

"Lovebirds! Here to pick up the pictures." The sound of his Italian accent was thick and echoing around the room.

"Yes, we are," Liam answered.

"Follow me." I looked around as Liam pulled me after him. Leonardo led us down a hallway that was lined with gorgeous photos of sunsets, flowers, people, and stars. Every single one was so beautiful

41

I just wanted to stop and look at them all day. Leonardo was very talented. If our pictures looked as good as the wedding ones lining the walls, I would be beyond happy. "Okay, here they are."

We came to a stop in front a huge counter that had more than a dozen of our engagement photos spread out on it. Dropping my hand from Liam's, I reached for the first one I saw. It was the one where Liam and I kissed. My breath hitched in my throat at how amazing we looked. The lighting was perfect and glowed around us as Liam held me up. My leg was popped in the air, my hands gripping his shoulders, my hair framed around his face, almost blocking it. I softly set it down and gently reached for another. I was afraid of ruining it. This one was the both of us at the lake. Leonardo snapped the picture just as I laughed. Liam was saying that Leo was his side babe. My head was thrown back while my hands gripped his, down between us. Liam was looking straight at me with a loving smile on his face.

The way he was staring at me while I laughed made my heart beat faster. It was the look of someone in love. I had seen Tom from the club look at his girlfriend Kendra the same way. The lake in the background looked amazing, and the sun was shining straight down at us, wrapping us in almost a cocoon of light. Smiling down at the picture, I moved onto the next one and grinned wider at the photo of all of us holding the boys' shirts open, revealing the super hero shirts. It turned out perfect! All three boys were looking down at their chests while Julie, Lennon, and I looked at the camera. All the pictures looked amazing, and I loved every single one. We could only pick two to go in the newspaper, and the decision was going to be tough. When I looked at each of the pictures of Liam and me, the look on our faces as we stared at each other made me smile in response. We looked good together; I wasn't going to lie.

"We need two photos. What ones do you like, Jenna?" Liam asked a few minutes after we both looked at all of them.

"Only two?" Leonardo interrupted. He sounded almost offended.

"For the paper. The rest we will use for invitations," Liam explained.

"I like this one." I pointed to the one by the lake with me laughing. "And this one," I said shyly, pointing to the one of us kissing.

"I do too." With a nod from Liam, Leonardo started packing up our photos in a big white box, leaving out the two we needed to drop off. Once everything was packaged up, Leonardo practically shooed us out. Shaking our heads at each other, we got in the car and headed to drop off our pictures. I was nervous about everyone in New York knowing that we were engaged. With Liam being who he was, I wouldn't be surprised if I got a lot of backlash from this. Women were smitten with Liam, and finding out he was engaged to some random girl wasn't going to go over well.

"We just have to go inside to the editor and drop these off. Then we can go," Liam said once we pulled up in front of *The New York Times* building. Nodding and taking a deep breath, I stepped out of the car. I automatically slipped my hand into Liam's, and we headed inside. It already felt natural, holding his big hand with my small one. I felt safe, like he was my rock.

Blushing under the looks everyone was sending our way, I leaned into Liam's side, wanting to disappear. I hated attention, but being with Liam, it came with the deal. I hated when people stared at me like I was some experiment under a microscope, waiting to be poked and examined. As Liam spoke to a lady at the front desk, I discreetly looked around and found a handful of people gawking at us, mostly women. I could hear them whispering to each other, asking who I was and why would a girl like me be with a guy like Liam. I felt small under their gaze, but I didn't want to show them how I felt. I straightened my back and turned away from their judging stares.

Walking to the elevator, I held my head up and ignored the whispers and looks. My grip tightened on Liam's hand until the doors of the elevator closed, cutting off the faces of people in the lobby. I let out a breath I didn't know I was holding.

"Don't listen to them," Liam whispered down at me even though we were the only ones in the closed space. I nodded and shot him a weak smile. I'd had plenty of people say things about me to my face and behind my back, but it never got any easier. There would always be a small part inside of me that agreed with everything they said, and it hurt, knowing it was true. I'd heard plenty of times that you shouldn't care what people think of you, but how do you do that when you think the exact same things they do?

"Liam Stanford here to see Mr. Parsons," Liam said as we came out of the elevator. The eyes of the girl behind the desk widened, and she opened her mouth like a fish gasping for water. She seemed star-struck by Liam and his looks.

"Uh, h-he is right in there," she stuttered, pointing to a door behind her. Thanking her, we walked to the door and inside.

"Mr. Parsons, I'm Liam Stanford, and this is Jenna Howard. I spoke with you on the phone earlier." Liam shook hands with the guy. He looked older, about late sixties, with a bald head and a beer belly.

"Oh yes, it is very nice to meet you," Mr. Parsons said enthusiastically. He gestured for us to sit down in front of his desk. "So this is your lovely fiancé." The way he was looking at me made my skin crawl. His beady little eyes stared at me as if he was undressing me. Used to guys doing that, I narrowed my eyes at him.

"We are here to drop off a few pictures so you can run them in the paper tomorrow about our engagement," Liam cut in, ignoring Mr. Parsons' remark about me. From the corner of my eye, I saw Liam clenching his jaw.

"We would be more than happy to put it in our paper. People are going to be surprised seeing that you are engaged, and to a very beautiful woman." I squirmed in my seat under his gaze.

"Here. We'd better get going." Liam threw the packet with our photos in them on his desk before standing up. I could tell Mr. Parsons was getting on his nerves as well. Following his lead, I stood up. I felt the ugly fat man's eyes on me, and I turned and caught him staring straight at my ass. Not caring anymore, I slammed my hand down on his desk. I pushed away the pain that was radiating up my arm as I glared at him.

"If you keep staring at my ass, I will come over there and pull your dick right off. Then I will leave you to explain to your *wife* that you are a disgusting pig who gets his jollies looking at young engaged women," I hissed at him. With a death glare at him, I moved away from his desk, grabbing Liam's hand and pulling him out of the room with me. As we passed by the girl at the front, I looked over at her. "I suggest you find another job instead of working for a dick who can't keep it in his pants." The girl's jaw hit the floor, and I entered the elevator.

It felt great finally saying something to someone as disgusting as that man. Working at the bar and having guys undress you with their eyes and say crude things to you was terrible, but not being able to say anything back was worse. We were just supposed to ignore them, unless they got handsy. Then one of the guards like Tom would come over. I grinned to myself as we rode the elevator down.

"Damn, I didn't know you had that in you," Liam said suddenly. I looked over at him and saw him staring at me with a look of awe and almost fear. "Remind me to never get on your bad side. I want to keep my balls attached." I laughed along with him.

"Sorry, I couldn't let it slide. I've dealt with plenty of guys like him at the club, and it felt great to finally say something back."

"Men like him really stared and said stuff to you while you worked?"

"Of course. Working at a strip club, you are more than likely to get looked at, get commented on, and sometimes touched. Comes with the territory," I said, shrugging.

"That's not right," Liam said, his voice hard.

"It's fine. We had guards stationed around if things got out of hand. It's not a big deal."

"I cannot believe you worked there," he muttered softly, but I still heard him. The elevator dinged, the doors opening. Leaving the lobby, we walked toward the car. "Let's get something to eat. I'm starving."

Liam flashed me a grin, and we slid into the car. He immediately took off down the street.

Chapter Four

The rest of the week flew by, and before I knew it, it was the day of the Benefit. Lennon was with me the entire week and kept going over everything I would need to know, from where the event was being held to who was going to attend. I learned everything about every person, who their family was, and what their company did. I was still in shock at myself for memorizing all the information in under a week, as were Liam and Lennon.

Since the Benefit started at seven and it was one now, I had plenty of time to get ready. The more time passed, the more nervous I got. This was our first appearance together, and after everyone seeing our engagement photos in the paper Wednesday, I knew we were going to be swarmed by the paparazzi. The morning our photos were released in the paper, our house was swarmed by people with cameras waiting for one of us to leave. My phone started blowing up with followers and messages from random people. Some were people saying how lucky I was to be marrying Liam, and then there were others calling me names and saying I wasn't good enough for him. By noon, I had over a thousand friend requests on Facebook and over twenty thousand followers on Instagram. It had been Lennon's idea to get Instagram the other day. I had only posted one picture and only because Lennon made me.

I was shocked at how many people wanted to be my friend and all the messages I was receiving. I didn't think being with Liam would be such a big ordeal. If I thought things were going to calm down, I was mistaken.

This entire week had to be the best one so far. Liam and I were getting along really well. Every night he would come home at five and help me make dinner. While we cooked we'd joke around and shoot remarks at one another. I hadn't known Liam could be sarcastic. Just yesterday we bickered back and forth over if a tomato was a fruit or a vegetable. Of course I thought it was a fruit, but he said vegetable. Over the last few days we had gotten into a routine. We would both cook, and he would wash the dishes while I dried them. Then, afterwards, we would sit on the couch together and watch whatever was on. I wouldn't admit it out loud, but I really enjoyed our time together lately. Liam was definitely a different guy than when I first met him a month ago.

I was currently in the library again, trying to finish *Twilight* before we left. I had to force myself to sit still instead of pacing the length of the house, nervous about tonight. I was actually enjoying the book and knew I would be reading the rest of the series in no time. It wasn't my favorite series, but it was good.

After Liam and I had had dinner the other day, we dropped off the photos and headed to a Barnes and Noble. The moment we walked in, I immediately headed to the young teen section, loving the books there. I could have spent hours there, but having Liam with me, I didn't want to make him wait. Of course, like every book lover, I found so many books I really wanted but didn't have the money to buy them all. Liam saw that I wanted the entire series of *The Mortal Instruments* and practically forced me to let him get them for me. He literally grabbed them from my hand and went to the cash register and paid for them before I even caught up to him. Now I was hoping to finish my current series so I could start on those.

I tried concentrating on my book but my thoughts kept drifting to tonight and to next week. Liam's mother, Lily, called me yesterday to tell me about how she had already started on the wedding plans. She wanted to get together sometime next week so we could discuss a theme, invitations, the date, and some other things. The thought of already starting on the wedding plans made my stomach knot up. Plus being alone with his mother, I was afraid I would say something I shouldn't. I had the tendency to ramble in awkward situations.

"You're in here again," Liam said suddenly. I jumped in my seat and looked up. My book tumbled into my lap. I hadn't really been paying attention to it anyways.

"Yeah, sorry, just being in here helps me feel

relaxed."

"I know exactly what you mean. I come in here when I'm not working," he said, coming into the room and taking a seat next to me on a chair.

Over these last few days my opinion of Liam had changed. He wasn't that cold, rude person anymore. He was nicer to me, almost attentive. Liam was starting to be the guy that Lennon kept telling me about. With him being so nice to me, something inside of me was starting to shift, and I didn't know how to react. When we were sitting at the table eating dinner together, he would tell me stories about him, Blake, and Lennon when they were little. That made my heart and stomach flutter. I would sit there listening to him and staring at his face as he grinned at the memories. There was something so enchanting about Liam. I don't know what it was, but it drew me in like gravity.

"Shouldn't you be getting ready for the Benefit?" Liam asked.

"I'm waiting for Lennon. I have strict instructions to not do anything until she gets here, in case I ruin it," I said, rolling my eyes.

"Definitely listen to her. She can be scary when she wants to be," he admitted, laughing softly. "She's made Blake cry."

"She made Blake cry!" I said, grinning and sitting up, wanting to hear more. "How?"

"He won't admit it because it has happened several times. One was during our junior year of college. He kept going on about how women shouldn't be president, stuff like that, and Lennon didn't like what he was saying so she kneed him in his balls. Then another time was when he had a bet going on with another guy playing pool, and, Lennon being Lennon, she had to butt in to distract Blake so he would lose. I don't think I have seen him cry that hard." Liam laughed and shook his head at the memory.

"Sounds like something Lennon would do, actually." I grinned at the story. "Can I ask you a question about them?"

"Sure." He turned his head and looked at me.

"Why aren't they together? It is plain as day that they like each other, a lot."

"How do you know they like each other?"

"Anyone with eyes can see it. They both look at each other like they are the moon to their sun," I said, giving him a look.

"Don't ask me why they aren't together. Blake has liked her since we were in high school. Not too sure about Lennon though, but it's clear she likes him just as much."

"You've never tried to get them together?"

"No, I've always figured they would work it out on their own." He shrugged. I got an idea, and I smiled almost evilly in my head. My goal from now until the deal was over was to get Blake and Lennon together. Someone deserved to be happy after this, even if those two wouldn't admit their feelings. They needed help, and I was going to be the one to provide it. "What is that look for? You are not thinking of doing something, are you?" Liam asked. He sent me a look that said I should stay out of it.

"I'm not going to do anything," I lied, waving my hand at him.

"I don't believe you." He narrowed his eyes at me. I put on an innocent smile. You would think he would approve of my idea of getting his two friends together, after they'd spent years of pining after one another. "Jenna," he warned.

"What did you do now, Jenna?" I heard Lennon ask, which interrupted my staring contest with Liam. I shot Liam a triumphant smile and turned to look at Lennon.

"Oh, nothing. Should we start getting ready?" I asked to change the subject.

"Yep, we have a lot to do." Lennon nodded, holding up a bag probably filled with five different dresses, a big bag overflowing with makeup even though I had some, and another bag with God knew what.

"Way to say I am ugly," I muttered, standing up and putting my book on the table.

"This conversation isn't over, Jenna," Liam said from behind me. Looking over my shoulder, I smirked at him before following Lennon out the door, ignoring the fact that he was looking at my backside.

***

Two and a half hours later, I emerged from the closet. Lennon didn't want me to look at my reflection until she was completely done, so I had to change in the closet. The dress we ended up picking was a beautiful, simple strapless red number. It flowed down to the ground, swishing around my feet. I loved it for its simplicity and gorgeousness.

The other options Lennon had were beautiful too, especially a deep purple one, but they felt too fancy or prom-like for an event such as this.

"Can I look now?" I asked, standing in the middle of the room.

"Not yet. Put these heels on, then let me add a few things. Then I will be done, I promise," she said, handing me a pair of black five-inch heels that had red on the bottom. I didn't know anything about fashion, but I knew these heels were expensive. Taking a seat on the bed, I moved the dress hem aside and slid the super high heels on. When I stood up, I wobbled before getting my balance. Tonight was going to be interesting. I had never walked in heels like this, and I knew I was going to make a fool out of myself.

I stood still for Lennon as she moved around me. Looking at the clock next to my bed, I saw it was a few minutes after six. My heart rate started to pick up. Taking a few deep breaths, I tried to calm my heart, chanting in my head that it was all going to be okay.

"Okay, here is the last touch," Lennon said. She came to a stop in front of me. In her hand was my engagement ring. Sliding it on my ring finger, I smoothed my hands down my dress.

"Do I look okay?" I asked, biting my bottom lip.

"See for yourself." She moved to the side, allowing me to see myself for the first time. With wobbly legs I walked to the mirror, and my green eyes widened at my reflection. Lennon was literally a genius when it came to makeup and hair.

My face was lightly spread with concealer,

hiding my little flaws and freckles on my nose. A little bit of pink blush graced my cheeks, and my lips were painted a bright red that matched my dress. Lennon had added on some of those fake eyelashes to my eyes, but I could only tell because I felt her do it. A light bronze-color eye shadow made my green eyes look like they had brown in them. After looking at my face, I saw my blonde hair was slightly curled at the bottom and hung down around my shoulders and framed my face. It was simple yet perfect.

"I look…amazing," I said finally. She made me look so beautiful I almost didn't recognize myself. I didn't look like the plain old Jenna. Instead I looked prettier and more confident. "Lennon, you are seriously gifted." I turned and smiled at her.

"Oh I know," she said, flipping her brown hair over her shoulder.

"Why aren't you coming tonight? I am going to be alone!" I said for the hundredth time since I'd started getting ready.

"Because I'm not some big business person, nor do I work at Stanford Industries. And I would rather sit at home alone than be at that party."

"That makes me feel so much better about going," I said sarcastically.

"Don't worry, Jenna, you will be fine. You know who is who and what they do. I know you can do this, and Liam will be with you all night too," Lennon said, putting a hand on my shoulder. "I have faith that you will make it out alive." I laughed, glad she could make the situation less serious.

"Thank you, Lennon." I sent her a grateful smile.

"No problem." A knock on the door interrupted us. I knew it was Liam and gulped, smoothing the dress once again. I was worried about Liam's reaction to seeing me. "I know, I know. We are done," Lennon said, opening the door. "Keep your mouth closed, okay?" she said before opening the door wide open and revealing Liam. He was dressed in a simple black and white suit that fit his frame perfectly. His brown hair was slicked back, making him look utterly sexy. I noticed he was wearing a red tie, the same color as my dress. When I looked over at Lennon, she smirked at me. She clearly told him what color I was wearing while I was changing.

As I was looking over him, he was doing the same to me. His mouth was wide open, and his eyes were wide as he took in my outfit. I shifted under his gaze, feeling self-conscious.

"Would you two stop eye-raping each other? You need to get going," Lennon snapped at us. Liam blinked, almost confused.

"Jenna, you...uh, you look great," Liam said, rubbing the back of his neck, not really looking at me. I ducked my head and grinned.

"Thank you." I blushed.

"I got you something," he said and walked toward me. I looked up, surprised. "Turn around." Doing as he said, I stood with my back facing him. I felt his hand move my hair over my shoulder and shivered as his fingertips brushed against my neck. A minute later I saw something being lowered over me and felt Liam clipping a lock. I looked down and saw a simple necklace with a diamond-encrusted heart draped above my chest. I brought my hand up and ran a finger over it, touched that he got me a necklace. Knowing Liam, the diamonds were real.

"It is beautiful," I said softly. I felt Liam rub his fingers against the base of my neck before he withdrew his touch, taking the warmth with him. Turning around, I looked up at him. "Thank you."

"It looks perfect on you," he said, staring into my eyes. I didn't know how long we stood there staring at one another until a loud cough made us look away. I swallowed and looked over at Lennon, who was standing there with a hand on her hip.

"Horny birds, let's go." Liam shook himself before nodding and holding his arm out for me to take. Smiling softly, I laced my arm through his and headed to the door. As I passed Lennon, she handed me a small clutch that she must have gotten ready when I wasn't looking. She winked at me and watched us walk toward the front door.

Instead of taking one of Liam's cars, a limo idled in front of the house. I stared at it with wide eyes. I had never been in a limo before. With my arm inside of Liam's, I followed behind him and tried to gracefully slide into the car, but of course that didn't happen. I practically fell face first. Thank God the dress was long, or I would have flashed Liam.

The whole ride to the Benefit I played with my fingers, trying to calm my nerves. I was not looking forward to meeting a lot of new people and having them stare at me like I was dirt on the bottom of their shoes.

"Jenna, you are going to do great. Just ignore what anyone says," Liam said, placing his hand on top of mine to stop my fiddling. I nodded and took a deep breath. *Jenna, you can do this.* "I will be by your side the entire time." He shot me an encouraging smile. The car came to a stop a second later. The driver got out and headed around to open our door. Outside the window beside Liam's head, I could see camera flashes going off like mad. "Just breathe, Jenna," Liam said softly into my ear.

The car door opened, and he sent me one last smile before sliding out. Instantly, the sounds of yelling and clicking of cameras reached my ears. Taking one last deep breath, I grabbed Liam's hand as he held it out for me. Praying that I wouldn't fall and make a fool out of myself, I got out of the car and straightened up. Immediately, blinding flashes of light hit both of us. I gripped Liam's hand tightly with my shaking one. I let him pull me alongside him.

With my free hand I gripped the bottom of my dress so I wouldn't step on it. My head whipped in different directions as people called our names. Flashes of light blinded me for a minute, and I gripped onto Liam's hand harder.

"Almost there," he whispered down at me. Yes, even in five-inch heels I was still shorter than he was. Lennon's voice echoed in the back of my mind as we walked toward the door, telling me to smile. I forced one on my lips so people could take photos of us and not think I wasn't happy or something. Thankfully a minute later we reached the door and walked through it, leaving all the yelling and flashing behind us. I let out a breath I didn't know I was holding and leaned against Liam.

"You did good, Jenna," he said and smiled down at me. I smiled back, feeling slightly better. Knowing that Liam was here next to me and not going anywhere made me feel better. He squeezed my hand reassuringly before we made our way deeper inside of the building, toward where the Benefit was being held. The moment we entered the room, it seemed everyone stopped what they were doing to look at us. I felt everyone's gaze scrutinizing me. Not wanting to let them get to me, I held my head up and swallowed my nerves.

As we moved around the room, I noticed there were at least one hundred people here. All the men were dressed in expensive-looking suits, and next to them their wives were in probably more expensive gowns and jewelry. The women looked so fancy and rich, affirming Lennon's teachings. She and Liam were right. These people could pick you up and eat you without so much as batting an eyelash. I noticed most of them looked around the room with a snotty look upon their faces as they judged everyone, even their so-called *friends.*

All along the walls surrounding the ballroom were paintings, sculptures, and other items, along with what looked like clipboards with stuff written on them. I briefly learned what the Benefit was about, but I was more concerned knowing who was who.

"Everything here can be auctioned off to the highest bidder. People can write down their price for a trip to Paris or something on those clipboards."

Liam gestured with his head as we passed them.

"But can't these people afford to go any day they want?" I whispered.

"Yes, but this is for a special cause. Being invited here, they are expected to make some effort to buy or donate. We are raising money to help the children's hospital here in New York. The money will help the hospital try to find a cure for various illnesses, as well as expand and get more doctors needed for the children." I stared up at him in awe. I didn't know he was such a giver and passionate about helping others, especially children. It was a great cause, and knowing that Liam's family's company was hosting the Benefit made me feel proud to know him.

"Liam Stanford! It is great to see you again," I heard a loud, booming voice call from in front of us. Looking away from Liam, I saw a burly man coming toward us. He stood a good two inches taller than Liam and had quite a gut to him. His face had a slight red glow to it, hinting he has already started drinking, even though it was a little bit after seven. The man was a big guy, but something about him seemed jolly.

"Kenneth, it is nice to see you as well." Liam dropped my hand to shake the man's.

"And this must be your fiancé. Hello, love, I am Kenneth Poltz," he said, sticking his hand out to me. I sent him a smile and shook his hand.

"Hello, I am Jenna Howard."

"Wow, she is a pretty little thing. Good catch, boy." Kenneth smacked Liam's shoulder roughly. "Honey, come meet Liam's fiancé," he said over his shoulder. Moving to the side, he revealed a beautiful, tall, brunette woman. She looked to be in her late forties but still gorgeous. Her hair was in a curled bun, and she was wearing a deep blue dress that highlighted her bright blue eyes. She looked like she was of Hispanic descent.

"Hello, I am Maria." She smiled kindly at me. I instantly felt relaxed around these two.

"Hi." I awkwardly smiled back at her.

"Kenneth owns one of the biggest stores in America," Liam said. I nodded, remembering hearing of him.

"That is impressive," I commented. The sound of Liam's name being called made us look in the other direction.

"I'm sorry, but my fiancé and I better go and see some other people. We will be back to talk, Kenneth and Maria," Liam said regretfully. I could tell he would rather stay here and talk to the Poltz instead of going around to everyone else.

"Don't worry, boy, we aren't going anywhere. We want to learn more about your lovely girl." He grinned at me, which earned an eye roll from his wife. Sending me a smile, she let me know she was used to her husband saying such things. I smiled back at them and trailed behind Liam as he led me to a new group of people.

For the next hour we went from group to group, meeting different people. I couldn't be more thankful that Liam had Lennon teach me about them. At first introduction most of them stared at me weirdly, like I was some bimbo, but when I congratulated them on a business deal or said

61

something about their business, they acted differently. Well, that was the men. After they checked me out they were fine, but their wives were another story. Most of the ones we met looked down at me rudely and scoffed whenever I talked. To say I wanted to strangle them was an understatement. But since I couldn't, I just kept ignoring them and talking to their husbands, making the wives even madder at me.

As we drifted from group to group, I felt stares following me the entire time. It had only been an hour and I was already fed up with these people. At first I thought I wouldn't be able to handle this, but now I wanted more than anything to yell at everyone to stop staring and mind their own damn business. After years of being talked about behind my back, I was done with people doing so. I didn't care if these people thought they were all high and mighty.

My feet were starting to hurt, and my mouth was hurting and getting dry from talking too much. After breaking away from yet another group, I looked around, realizing there were still a lot of people to talk to.

"Um, Liam?" I asked, tugging on his hand.

"Yes?" He immediately looked down at me. "Is something wrong?" His voice was filled with worry. Smiling softly, I shook my head

"No, I was just wondering if I could get a drink."

"Of course. No alcohol," he said.

"Wait, how did you know I don't like alcohol?" I asked, confused. I hadn't told him I didn't like it.

"I saw your face at my parents' when we had

wine, and whenever we eat you only ever have water," he explained. I stood there, shocked. "I'll go get you a water. You just stay right here." Nodding, I watched him leave. When I looked around, I saw a few people duck their heads, not wanting to be caught staring. Feeling awkward standing there by myself, I opened my clutch and grabbed my phone. When I pressed on the home button, I saw Lennon had texted me an hour ago wishing me luck and asking me to tell her how it was tomorrow. I also got a text from Sophia asking how things were. Sending them both a quick reply, I put my phone back and glanced up, looking for Liam.

Thinking he got held up, I looked around for his mop of brown hair and instantly froze. I stared wide-eyed at the woman standing not even three feet in front of me. Her blonde hair was shorter than when I had last seen it and half pulled up. Her face was, of course, older, but had aged well. She still looked the same to me. I watched as she laughed, and then I looked around as my last shred of doubt vanished. A pair of familiar green eyes glanced over at me, then looked away.

I felt like everything around me vanished, leaving only me and her. My heart shattered and dropped to the pit of my stomach. The woman in front of me I thought I'd never see again. Hell, I was hoping to never see her again. Old memories I had pushed deep down rushed up and captured me. My eyes welled up with tears as I stared at her smiling and lacing her hand through a man's. I watched as the man smiled down lovingly at her and leaned down to kiss her lips.

Even though it had been fourteen years, everything about her was familiar. She looked the exact same as she did all those years ago when she left me on the doorstep of a house, clutching my teddy bear. She kept glancing around her but didn't seem to recognize me. All different kinds of emotions rolled around inside me, from anger to sadness to hate. My breath got stuck in my chest, and I felt myself breathing heavily trying to get some air.

"Jenna," I heard Liam say, but I couldn't tear my eyes away from the woman. "Jenna, what's wrong?" he asked.

I didn't hear anything he said after that as I stared at the woman who abandoned me when I was five. I stared at my mother. I never thought I would see her again.

Chapter Five

"Mommy!" I cried, jumping off the bench and running toward her, my blonde hair flying behind me and my backpack bouncing between my shoulder blades. The moment I reached her, I clutched her legs, wrapping myself almost like a koala bear around them.

"Hi, baby," she said, squatting down to my level. I wrapped my arms around her neck, burying my face into her shoulder and breathing in her scent. "I am sorry I am late. I had some things to do." She pulled away and smiled at me.

I had been sitting on a bench in front of my elementary school waiting for my mom to come and get me. All the other kids left with their parents almost two hours ago. The longer I sat outside the school, the more I worried she wouldn't come back to get me. Being alone without your parents is scary when you're only old enough to be in kindergarten.

"I missed you, Mommy," I said, looking up at her as she stood up. Her blonde hair was up in a bun, and she was dressed the way she usually did—

65

in a pair of worn blue jeans and a t-shirt.

"I did too, baby. Remember, Jenna, I will never leave you. I will always come back."

I gasped for air, my whole body frozen and my feet planted firmly on the floor. My mother looked the same as when I'd last seen her. Everything that I pushed to the back of my mind concerning my mother came rushing up, overwhelming me. A big masculine body moved in front of me, blocking my mother from my line of sight.

"Jenna." The sound of my name being whispered above me and the feeling of a pair of hands on my shoulders made me blink. Looking up, I met Liam's blue eyes. I didn't know why, but seeing him staring down at me with worry and almost fear in his eyes made my own eyes water.

"I…I n-need air," I choked out. Seeing the state I was in, he only nodded and let go of my shoulders and grabbed one of my hands before pulling me after him. My whole body felt numb as Liam led me past groups of people talking. The moment we stepped out on a balcony, I took in mouthfuls of air as Liam shut the door behind us. I went over and gripped the railing that ran around the edge of the balcony, panting and trying to force back my tears.

That woman didn't deserve my tears. She didn't deserve anything from me. That stopped the minute she left me at the foot of some house in the middle of the night. That woman was not my mother. What kind of person, what kind of mother, would abandon her own daughter? And here I was fourteen years later, struggling to make ends meet, when she was here with some rich guy. How the hell did this even happen? After all this time, how could she be here, of all places? How could she be standing here with some rich guy, pretending like she didn't leave her daughter on the streets fourteen years ago?

Two tears fell away from my eyes. My whole body was starting to shake. I wanted to sob, but I wouldn't permit myself. All I wanted to do was get out of here and run home, but I knew I couldn't. I had to stay here for Liam. Fighting back another sob, I gripped the edge of the balcony tighter. My knuckles turned white. I bit my bottom lip until I tasted blood. A few more tears leaked out of my eyes when I felt a pair of arms wrapping themselves around my waist, pulling me back against something hard and warm.

I knew it was Liam, and I sunk back against him, closing my eyes tightly, but that didn't help. All I could see what my mom in front of me, throwing her head back, laughing and smiling at whatever the stranger on her arm was saying.

"Jenna, what's wrong?" Liam asked in a whisper by my ear.

"My m-mother is here," I whispered back.

"What do you mean your mother is here?" I heard his tone suddenly change from soft to hard.

"S-she was right in front of me when you left to get us a drink. She was with a man." I opened my eyes and stared out at the river and the city. "How can she be here, Liam? I thought I'd never see her again, and yet here she is." More tears ran down my cheeks, and I knew my makeup was starting to get ruined.

"Jenna," Liam said, his voice once again soft as he gently turned me around by my waist. "Let's get you out of here." He brought his hands up and cupped my cheeks. With the pads of his thumbs, he wiped away the tears coming down my cheeks.

"What? No, Liam, we can't go. This is your benefit party," I said, looking up into his eyes.

"I do not care. They will be fine without me. I don't want you to face that woman." I didn't know if it was because I was so emotional at that moment, but him saying that made my heart beat faster. Liam cared enough about me to leave his company's benefit party so I wouldn't have to face my mother.

"But—"

"No, we are leaving," he interrupted me. He gave me a firm look while wiping his thumbs under my eyes, cleaning my running mascara off. "Let's go." Giving me a nod, he grabbed my hand gently with his and started for the door. With his hand in mine I felt better, like I could face whatever was ahead. Pushing down all my feelings for a moment, I followed Liam, practically hiding behind him. He was going to be my shield to get out of here. Just as we made it halfway across the room, someone had to stop us.

"Liam!" a man said. I pressed tightly against Liam's side and peeked up through my hair at the man. Instantly I froze and clenched Liam's hand tighter. It was the man who was with my mother. Up close he looked be in his forties, same as her. His brown hair was cut short, and his black tux fit him pretty well.

"Martin," Liam said, glancing down at me,

confused, when I clenched his hand.

"It is great to see you. We haven't talked in a while," Martin replied. The moment I heard his name, I cocked my head to the side, trying to remember where I heard that name before. "My wife keeps asking about you as well." Martin kept talking to Liam as if I wasn't there.

"Martin, this is my fiancé, Jenna," Liam said, cutting him off. The man's attention turned to me, and I leaned more into Liam's side. I knew my makeup was messed up from crying.

"Hello. I guess I better introduce myself. I am Martin Brotherson." He stuck his hand out to me. Suddenly the name clicked, and I had to force myself not to run away.

Stupid Jenna! Why didn't you figure it out before? I shouted inwardly at myself. Brotherson was one of the names Lennon had me learn. His wife's name was Karen, and they had two kids, thirteen-year-old twins, away at boarding school. At the time, I didn't realize that his wife had the same name as my mother, Karen. But now, having seen them together, I knew she really was married to him and had other kids. *I have other siblings.*

"Honey…oh, it is Liam Stanford," an all-too-familiar voice said. A hand wrapped itself around Martin's arm, and my mother's face came into view. She was looking at Liam with a wide smile, not having seen me yet. I pushed myself even more into Liam's side, wanting to melt into him. My mother was *right* in front of me!

"Karen," Liam said, oblivious to who she was. A strangled sound escaped my lips before I could stop it, making everyone turn to me. Eyes the same green as mine stared at me. I could tell right then that she did not recognize me at all. There was no spark of familiarity in her eyes. At that realization, my heart crumbled into a pile at my feet.

My hand tightened painfully around Liam's. I was certain I would break it. He looked down at me, but I couldn't keep my eyes off my mom. He must have gotten the hint or something, for he looked between Karen and me before his mouth thinned into a line.

The longer I stared at my mother, the angrier I became. Here she was standing in front of me, not even recognizing her own daughter! She was staring at me like the other women I had met that night, like I was beneath her. There was nothing in her face that showed she knew who I was or that she cared. Biting my tongue, I fought the urge to yell and cry at the same time.

"I am sorry, but my fiancé and I have to get going. It was nice seeing you again," Liam said, giving them a polite smile and nod. Thank God. Without waiting for their response, he was pulling me away from my mother and her husband.

I was in a daze the entire walk to the car and the drive home. I could hear and feel Liam talking to me and trying to get me to say something, but I couldn't. My body was here, but my mind wasn't. I used to think when I was younger, hell even just a few years ago, that whenever I would see my mom again—if she was even alive—I'd be happy, and she would recognize me. That dream went down the drain the moment I saw her. Never in a million

70

years did I think I would see that woman at an event with only rich people. And I never thought she would have another family. She had two kids! Two kids that I learned about before coming here.

Why would she do this? Why would she leave me when I was only five and start an entire new life? Why disappear and not take me with her? She left me on my own, left me to take care of myself. Left me to work two shitty jobs just to make ends meet. She even left me to make this decision to be with Liam. If it wasn't for her leaving me, I wouldn't have had to take this deal. I would be living a normal life: going to school, making friends, having someone to love me, and having someone to tell everything to.

The only reason I knew we were back home was when a pair of arms slid around me and lifted me out of the car. Being held bridal style, I laid my head against Liam's chest. For some reason, being held by Liam and knowing we were home, away from people's stares, made the tears I was holding back come rushing to the surface. Before I knew it, my body was wracked with sobs. My throat and chest tightened, my body almost folding in on itself. All of my repressed emotions were now coming out.

I was oblivious to Liam carrying me inside and up to his room. My tears were soaking Liam's suit jacket and shirt, but I couldn't stop the sobs. I didn't care if my makeup was running down my face or if I was ruining my hair or dress. All I could think about was my mother standing in front of me. The soft creak of the bed let me know Liam was now sitting down with me in his lap. Somehow I had turned myself around and was now straddling his lap with my arms wrapped tightly around his neck.

"Jenna, baby, it's okay," Liam said soothingly into my ear. I felt his hand softly move down my hair. I continued to cry as Liam whispered into my ear and rubbed my hair and back soothingly.

I was never really a crier. The most I ever cried was the day after my mother left me and I had to go to the orphanage. I must have cried myself out, because after that moment, I never once shed a tear. I didn't cry when I graduated high school and left my two "friends." I didn't cry when Carrie and Lea got adopted. I certainly didn't cry until I met Liam.

I didn't know how long I cried on him, but I finally calmed down, hiccupping silently. Liam stopped rubbing my back some time ago and was now just holding me against him. My eyes felt swollen, my throat raw. My body was slightly shaking but less than it had been before.

"Let's get you out of your clothes," he whispered, lifting me up. I was wrapped around his body like a koala bear, with my legs around his waist and arms around his neck. There was something about Liam that calmed me down.

The feeling of the counter against the back of my thighs made me unlock my legs from around Liam and sit on the countertop. I wanted to feel embarrassed as I sat there with tear-stained cheeks and red, swollen eyes, but I couldn't feel anything. I was completely numb. I was all cried out, and all I could do was sit there, watching Liam move around the bathroom.

"Do you want to take a bath?" Liam asked, looking over at me. His face was filled with compassion and what seemed like sadness. I almost nodded, but then I realized Liam would have to see me naked, so I shook my head. He nodded and headed for the sink. I watched as he grabbed a wash cloth and wetted it.

He came to a stop in front of me, spreading my legs so he could stand in between them. With softness I didn't think he possessed, he cupped my jaw in one hand and gently wiped my makeup off my cheek with the other. I didn't have it in me to tell him that that was not how you get makeup off, so I let him wash my face clean. He washed my face so softly I almost didn't feel it. Closing my eyes, I sighed as I felt my makeup slowly coming off, leaving me fresh-faced. A few minutes later, he went and washed the cloth before coming back with it clean to wipe my face once more. I couldn't help but open my eyes and look at him as he worked.

His expression was soft and concentrated as he wiped my face. I wanted to laugh at his intense focus, but it seemed my body didn't want me to. Our gaze suddenly locked, making him stop and stare at me. The urge to kiss him came over me once again. Liam lowered his head and laid his forehead against mine, his minty breath fanning across my face.

"I am sorry about your mother. I did not know she was Martin Brotherson's wife," he murmured softly. His tone was sincere as he looked at me.

"It is okay," I croaked. Clearing my throat, I spoke again. "I just…I can't believe she is here.

After all this time, she was still in New York, making a new life." I thought I was done crying but apparently not. My eyes flooded with tears once more. Saying it out loud made it more real, that I had seen her and that she wasn't a figment of my imagination. I looked away from Liam, willing my tears away.

"Jenna, look at me." With one finger, he lifted my chin until I was looking back at him. "I will not let that woman near you, okay? I will make sure she doesn't hurt you again," he said almost forcefully. He looked at me, waiting for my answer. The way he said it made my heart warm up. For some reason, I knew Liam meant what he said. He meant he would keep me safe.

"I…thank you," I whispered, nodding at him. Happy with my answer, he placed a gentle kiss on my forehead before stepping back.

"Let's get you changed." He held his hand out, waiting for mine. Without hesitation, I slid off the counter and put my hand in his. He led me out of the bathroom and toward his closet. I stared at his back. Liam was just confusing my feelings even more. "Here, you can put these on," he said, dropping my hand and reaching for something. Turning around, he handed me a big grey t-shirt and a pair of boxers.

"I can just go to my room," I said but silently hoped he would say no.

"No, you are staying in here tonight." His voice was firm. Inside I jumped with glee and nodded at him, taking the clothes. "I won't look." Turning his back to me, he looked in the other direction. The brief question of why couldn't he go back in the room for me to change crossed my mind, but I squashed it. Same with the question of me going to my room. If Liam wanted me here, then I was going to stay. Plus I didn't want to be alone, not right now.

I struggled with zipper on my dress and huffed, bending my arm at an awkward angle to unzip it. At the sound of my huff, Liam turned around. He saw my problem and moved behind me and laid his warm hands on my bare shoulders. Suppressing a shiver, I stood still as he slowly unzipped my dress. When I thought he was done, I moved forward but stopped when I felt his fingertip grazing up my spine and to my neck. My body felt like it was on fire as he softly ran his fingertips across my shoulders and neck, unclasping the necklace I had completely forgotten I was wearing. I felt his warm breath get heavy on my neck, and I bit my bottom lip. With a quiet groan I almost didn't hear, Liam pulled himself away from me and moved to stand in front of me with his back turned once more.

I shook my head at my hormones and quickly slipped out of my dress and heels into his big shirt and boxers. The shirt hung off of me but thankfully hid the fact I wasn't wearing a bra. Grabbing my dress, I held it in my arms.

"I am done." For some reason I felt like I had to whisper. Facing me, he grabbed my dress and heels in one hand. He grabbed my hand and tugged me after him. I didn't resist. Setting my clothes on a chair by the window in his room, he led me to his king-sized bed. As I swung my legs up on the bed, I glanced at the alarm clock on Liam's bedside table and saw it was only nine, but my body was exhausted. I almost moaned out loud when I lay back on the bed. It was so comfortable, way more than mine. "I am going to go change. Just lay down and relax."

Turning onto my side, I watched as Liam walked back to the bathroom. I looked up at the ceiling and tried to get my mind off of my mother. Liam's face popped into my mind, and I smiled softly. Him being so sweet and caring in the last hour just proved that he was different than when I first met him. I was thankful in this moment that Liam was here with me. If not, I would be home alone at my apartment crying myself to sleep. If it wasn't for this deal with Liam, I wouldn't have seen my mother, but I was kind of glad I did.

I was glad I saw that she was alive at least, even if she didn't recognize me. If you would have asked me two weeks ago, hell, even a week ago, I would say I regret taking this deal with Liam, but now it was different. I was glad I did it. This last week had been a great one, and being around Liam made me feel better. Yes, we got off on the wrong foot, but now we were getting along. Everything was slowly falling into place. Even though I did see my mother after fourteen years, I wouldn't change meeting Liam. I shouldn't even be thinking like that, but I was. Tonight just confirmed my thoughts.

When I heard the bed creaking and shifting, I looked over and was met with the sight of a beautiful tan muscular chest. Liam was shirtless and crawling into bed beside me. I gulped, staring at his toned stomach and forgetting about everything else. "What were you thinking about?" Liam asked, drawing my attention back to his face. Forcing a blush away from my cheeks, I swallowed.

"Just about my mother, that's all," I lied. Well, it was partly the truth.

"Don't think about her, Jenna. She doesn't deserve you." I smiled softly at him.

"Thank you, Liam. I am sorry we had to leave the Benefit. And that I cried all over your shirt," I mumbled.

"Don't worry about it. The Benefit is fine without me, and that shirt was old anyways," he said, waving it away and sending me a smile. The smile made me feel better. Just then, I yawned. After everything today, I was beyond exhausted. Stressing all day about the Benefit and then seeing my mother was very taxing. "Just go to sleep. I got you," Liam said, bringing his arms around me and drawing me toward him. I folded my body against his, putting my head on his chest. It felt nice, being held.

Letting out a sigh, I closed my eyes and breathed in the smell of Liam. I felt his hand rubbing my back and his head lying on top of mine. Glad that my face was hidden from him, I smiled and snuggled deeper against him. Before I knew it, I was drifting off to sleep. I barely heard Liam tell me goodnight.

Chapter Six

I woke up the next morning to swollen eyes and a scratchy sore throat. I snuggled deeper in the soft bed and sheets, ignoring the light streaming through the blinds. I tried to will my body back to sleep, but it didn't work. I was up now. I really hated being one of those people that once they were up they were up; there was no going back to sleep. With a groan, I rolled onto my back, bringing my comforter up and over my head.

As I lay there, a very nice manly smell wrapped itself around me. I breathed the scent in deeply, loving it. I stayed there, smelling the sheets like a weirdo, but what happened last night rushed to the front of my mind. I groaned even louder as I realized that seeing my mother was not something I had simply dreamed. I replayed everything in my mind, then sat up as I remembered I was in Liam's bed. The comforter fell to my lap as I looked around the room. Liam was nowhere in sight, but the sounds of plates clinking together let me know he was in the kitchen. Seeing as it was nine in the morning, I pushed the comforter away and swung out of the bed. I hadn't slept that well in a long time, and I was reluctant to leave the cozy bed.

I did my thing in the bathroom, but I winced at my reflection. My hair, which had been curled last night, was tangled and sticking up everywhere. My green eyes were red and swollen from crying so hard. At least I didn't have dried/ruined makeup on. I slowly made my way out of Liam's room and over to the kitchen. I walked in on the sight of Liam in nothing but a pair of shorts that hung low on his hips. His muscular back faced me, making my mouth suddenly dry. Liam was definitely out of my league.

Since I was not wearing any shoes or socks, I padded over to the bar quietly. When I pulled a chair out, it made a squeaking sound that made Liam whirl around, almost dropping the pan in his hands.

"You scared me," he said, trying to catch his breath.

"Sorry," I said sheepishly. He turned back around, giving me time to check out his well-toned backside. Watching Liam cook was very hot, to be honest. Something about a man that knew how to cook was seriously sexy. On top of already being sexy, Liam wasn't wearing a shirt, displaying his nice abs for me, making the whole situation a lot hotter than usual.

"Here you go, my lady," he said with an accent, bringing a smile to my face. When he set a plate in front of me, I had to keep myself from laughing. Liam had made me differently shaped pancakes. I could tell he really did try on them, but they looked like big batches of misshaped circles. One looked like a heart, but one side was larger than the other. All in all, it was the sweetest thing anyone had ever done for me.

"You made me pancakes."

"And apple juice, since I know you like that better than orange juice." He slid a glass in front of me. I looked at him, feeling absolutely touched.

"Liam…thank you," I said sincerely. No one had ever made this much of an effort for me before.

"It's no problem. I hope it tastes good." He slid into the chair beside me. I rolled my eyes at that, knowing it would even if it didn't look pretty. The next few minutes, we ate in silence. The breakfast was good, and I even got up to get extra.

"Liam, thank you for last night. You really didn't have to do that," I finally said. I needed to thank him for leaving his company's event for me and for taking care of me.

"Jenna, it is fine. Don't worry about it. I am happy to take care of you." He turned to me. "Don't even apologize for crying on me." His tone was firm. I knew it was useless saying anything else. "How about we do something today?" he suggested.

"I don't know. What could we do?" The idea of spending the whole day doing something fun with Liam sounded very appealing. His face lit up, and his mouth went wide in a grin.

"Don't worry, I got it figured out. It will definitely make you forget about your mother." The look on his face made me almost nervous.

"You're not going to take me to a strip club,

right? I've worked at one and have seen enough boobs and asses to last me an entire lifetime."

"No, just go get ready." He rolled his eyes at me before standing up and grabbing both of our plates.

"I can help do the dishes," I said, getting up after him. I didn't feel right leaving him to do them.

"Don't you need a while to get ready?" I sent him a look at that. As I stood beside him at the sink, I waited to start putting our dishes in the dishwasher. After we did the dishes, we both headed to our rooms to get ready.

The entire time I showered, I was grinning from ear to ear. For the first time in a long time, I felt relaxed, happy, and excited. Liam might have been an ass to me in the beginning, but now with him acting the way he was, I knew I would fall for him. I was already falling. I got dressed in my new pair of light blue skinny jeans and a teal-colored sweater. After brushing my teeth and putting a little bit of makeup on to hide my blotchy skin, I nodded at my reflection. I left my hair down, and it was starting to curl just a tad on the bottom. I added a swipe of pink lipstick and grabbed my brown lace-up boots and slipped them on. Deciding to leave my ring here today, I put my bag on my shoulder and left my room. I had no idea what Liam had planned, but I didn't want to risk losing or ruining my ring.

When I left my room, Liam came walking toward me. He looked me up and down, flashing me his pearly whites in a grin.

"Ready to go?" he asked. My mouth felt dry as I took in what he was wearing. Even in a simple grey t-shirt and a pair of low ride ripped blue jeans, he looked delicious.

"Yeah. What exactly are we doing?" I asked, tearing my eyes away from his body as we walked to the garage and into his Range Rover. This guy really had too many cars.

"It's a surprise." He wiggled his eyebrows at me.

"You're not planning on taking me somewhere to kill me, right?" I joked. When he didn't answer, my eyebrows shot up. "Liam, right?"

"If I wanted to kill you, I would have done it sooner. Too many people know who you are now," he said wickedly.

"Ha, you're too late!" I stuck my tongue out at him. "You wouldn't want to kill me anyways. I'm too amazing," I bragged.

"I wouldn't go that far," Liam teased, glancing over at me with a smile. Even though he was driving, I gently punched his shoulder.

A few minutes later, Liam pulled into a familiar parking lot. Turning to him, I grinned excitedly.

"We are at Fiesta Fun! Are we going to play mini-golf?" I asked. Before he could even answer, I stepped out of the car and around the front.

"Well, we can, if you want to. After. I was thinking of doing laser tag first," he said once he reached me.

"Laser tag! What are we waiting for? Come on!" Without thinking, I grabbed his hand and pulled him after me as I headed inside the building. Excitement overwhelmed any other feeling I had.

***

Liam

"Liam, calm down. I'm on my way right now," Lennon said through the phone. Jenna and I currently had about three hours until we had to be at the Benefit. I knew Lennon and knew that it would take a good three hours for her to get Jenna ready. I wasn't necessarily nervous about being late. I was just nervous about Jenna meeting a ton of people. I knew the kind of people that were going to be there tonight and did not want Jenna anywhere near them, but I had to take her with me.

"Just get here, okay?" I said, walking into the house.

"Calm your tits," was all she said before she hung up on me. I rolled my eyes, used to Lennon's weirdness, and headed deeper in the house. I walked into the living room expecting to find Jenna there, but no. After checking her room, I started calling her name. I headed up to the library, and I was not surprised to find her curled up in the chair with a book in her hands. She looked so adorable sitting there with her blonde hair tumbling around her face and her bottom lip sucked between her front teeth. I noticed she did that when she was deep in thought.

"You're in here again," I said, surprising her, making the book fall into her lap.

"Yeah, sorry. Just being in here helps me feel relaxed."

"I know exactly what you mean. I come in here when I'm not working," I said, walking into the room and taking a seat next to her. "Shouldn't you be getting ready for the Benefit?"

"I'm waiting for Lennon. I have strict instructions to not do anything until she gets here, in case I ruined it," she said, rolling her eyes. I laughed softly, knowing exactly what she meant.

"Definitely listen to her. She can be scary when she wants to be. She's made Blake cry."

"She made Blake cry?" she asked, eyes widening as she sat up in the chair. "How?"

"He won't admit it because it's happened several times. One time was during our junior year of college. He kept going on about how women shouldn't be president, stuff like that, and Lennon didn't like what he was saying, so she kneed him in his balls. Then, another time was when he had a bet going on with another guy playing pool, and, Lennon being Lennon, she had to butt in, distracting Blake so he would lose. I don't think I have seen him cry that hard before." I shook my head at the memory. One of the funniest moments we shared.

"Sounds like something Lennon would do, actually." She shook her head, laughing under her breath. "Can I ask you a question about them?" she asked a minute later.

"Sure." I turned my head and looked at her, starting to get worried.

"Why aren't they together? It is plain as day that they like each other, a lot."

"How do you know they like each other?" I mean, it wasn't like it was news, but Jenna had only met them twice. How could she know they liked each other?

"Anyone with eyes can see it. They both look at each other like they are the moon to their sun," she said, giving me a look like "duh".

"Don't ask me why they aren't together. Blake has liked her since we were in high school. Not too sure about Lennon though, but it's clear she likes him just as much." Blake had been head over heels in love with Lennon since I could remember. Of course, being a wimp, he never once did anything about it, even when Lennon had boyfriends and he would get jealous. If it were up to me, they would be dating by now.

"You've never tried to get them together?" she asked.

"No, I've always figured they would work it out on their own." I shrugged. I watched as her face morphed into a weird expression I'd never seen before. I could practically see the wheels turning in her head and knew she was thinking up something. "What is that look for? You are not thinking of doing something, are you?" I sent her a look to stay out of it. They could work it out themselves.

"I'm not going to do anything," she said, but I knew she was lying.

"I don't believe you." I narrowed my eyes at her. She put on an innocent smile, but I could see right through it. She was going to do something stupid and most likely get both of us in trouble with Blake and Lennon. "Jenna," I warned one last time.

"What did you do now, Jenna?" I heard Lennon ask, interrupting us staring at one another.

"Oh, nothing. Should we start getting ready?" Jenna said, turning away from me.

"Yep, we have a lot to do," I heard Lennon say, but I was still focused on Jenna.

"Way to say I am ugly," Jenna muttered under her breath. *Yeah, right.* She could never be ugly.

"This conversation isn't over, Jenna," I said. I saw them walk out of the room. She sent me a devious smirk, making something down below jump a little. She was a sexy fox, but she didn't know it. I stared after her until she was gone from my sight.

Ever since our engagement photos, Jenna and I had become closer. I was tired of acting rude toward her. Seeing her look at me with her doe-like blue eyes made it hard for me to be mean toward her. She didn't know how hard she was to resist. Yes, I had only known her for almost a month now, but she had gotten her claws inside of me. Everything she did was intoxicating to me. It literally was taking everything inside of me not to grab her and kiss the shit out of her.

With a groan at my thoughts, I stood up and headed to my room to take a cold shower. I could not go to the Benefit feeling like this. While Jenna got ready, I showered and slowly got ready myself, mentally playing out the Benefit the entire time. I wanted everything to go smoothly for Jenna and not let her get too overwhelmed. This was her first big event, and I knew how stressful and nerve-wracking it could be. When I was in high school and first started attending these with my father and mother, I was nervous about acting stupid in front of very important people or doing something that could hurt my family's company's reputation. But after attending so many events, I was now a pro and knew what to expect. The same people always went, so it would be no surprise to me.

All week Lennon had been teaching Jenna about everyone that was going to be there, and I was very impressed by how fast Jenna learned their names and businesses. When I first met Jenna in that sleazy strip club, I was actually considering taking back picking her. The whole week before I had spoken to her I had Matt, my driver, go to the club to scout out a girl. I knew going to a strip club was not the greatest choice, but I also knew the women there would be more likely to say yes because they needed the money. When Matt came back to me, he told me about this girl that looked young and seemed kind of feisty. He described Jenna to me, and for some odd reason, it made me want to go to the club and see her. So I did.

For three days, I went the club and watched Jenna from afar as she worked. Something about her sparked my interest. If she was some rich daddy's girl, she did a good job of hiding it. After seeing her the final night, I knew I would pick her. Maybe because she seemed like an easy target or that her innocence dragged me in, but I wanted her to say yes to my deal.

Now, a month later, we actually liked each other and were doing pretty well with our deal. Yes, she blabbed to her driver Garrett about our deal and it got out to the press, but I wasn't as angry as I thought I'd be. I mean, when I found out it was him that night, all I saw was red, but I wasn't mad at Jenna. Later, after I snapped at her, I felt guilty and wallowed in my bedroom the rest of the night. And I was glad that Garrett kid was out of the picture. I knew I wasn't around much, but I could tell the kid was taking a liking to her. He looked at her with lust in his eyes, something that Jenna was oblivious to. I hadn't known it then, but I was jealous that he was spending time with her and not me. He took her to get paint for the room and offered to help her. The day we "painted" the room was one of the best days I'd had in years.

I was so caught up in my thoughts I hadn't realized the time until I glanced over at my bedside table. We had thirty minutes to get there. When I say we had thirty minutes to be there, I meant thirty minutes so we could be fashionably late. It was better if we showed up later than others; that was what my father always told me. It showed people that you had other things you were doing or could be doing instead of being there. Plus it was our company hosting the event, so I could show up whenever I wanted.

Needing to get dressed, I quickly pulled on a crisp white button-up shirt and a pair of black dress pants. A few minutes ago Lennon had texted me saying Jenna was wearing a red dress, so I picked out a red tie to match. After tightening that on, I pulled on a black suit jacket before fixing my hair. Seeing that I looked good, I nodded at my reflection and grabbed the present I had gotten Jenna and left my room. Earlier in the week I had been driving by a jewelry shop on the way to work, and when I stopped at a red light I looked over. I could barely make anything out in the window, but something sparkling caught my attention. Instead of heading to work, I turned around and went to the store. A few minutes later I walked out with a beautiful yet simple heart necklace. It screamed "Jenna" to me, and I knew I had to get it.

When I came to a stop in front of her room, I straightened my tie and felt my pockets to make sure I had everything I needed for tonight. With one last deep breath, I knocked on the door and waited to be let in. I did not want to just barge in and get yelled at by Lennon. A second later, it was opened by the devil herself. I took a step inside and immediately froze. Jenna looked absolutely breathtaking. Even dressed in a simple strapless red dress she looked stunning. Her long blonde hair fell around her face, and her green eyes stared back at me. I could feel her eyes looking over me, and I was clearly doing the same. She looked better than I imagined.

"Would you two stop eye-raping each other? You need to get going," Lennon snapped at us, making my gaze break away from Jenna. I blinked a few times, trying to clear my mind.

"Jenna, you…uh, you look great." I stumbled over my words. Mentally, I slapped myself at how stupid I sounded. I'd never gotten flustered over a woman before.

"Thank you." She blushed, ducking her head down. I could see her cheeks turning a light pink.

"I got you something," I said, walking toward her. Her head snapped up in surprise. "Turn around." She did as I asked. Taking the necklace out of its case, I brought it down over her head and let it lay above her heart. After shutting the clasp, I briefly let my fingers rub the base of her neck before stepping away from her. I didn't want to do something stupid.

"It's beautiful," she whispered. "Thank you." Jenna turned to face me.

"It looks perfect on you." The necklace did look great on her. Hell, everything looked great on her. She could wear a pair of sweats to the Benefit and I would think she looked amazing.

"Horny birds, let's go," Lennon said and coughed loudly. I forced myself to take my eyes off of Jenna and held my arm out for her to take. I smiled as she laced her arm through mine. As we walked away, I looked over my shoulder and mouthed a "thank you" to Lennon before leading Jenna to the front of the house and to the limo waiting for us. I watched from the corner of my eye as Jenna nervously played with her fingers. I knew she was worried and didn't really know what to say or do. It had been a *long* time since I had comforted a woman who wasn't my mother, my sister, or Lennon.

"Jenna, you are going to do great. Just ignore what anyone says," I said as I felt the car slow down. "I will be by your side the entire time." I shot her a smile, hoping to calm her nerves. I laid one of my hands on top of hers, squeezing it softly. "Just breathe, Jenna," I said softly into her ear. Giving her a nod and an encouraging smile, I slid out of the car as the driver opened the door for me. Immediately I was swarmed with flashing lights and yells from the paparazzi. Turning around, I held out my hand for Jenna. She got out of the car and looked shocked as the lights flashed like crazy.

I gripped her hand and led her past the paparazzi, and the entire time they were yelling at us for interviews. I felt Jenna grip my hand tighter, and I returned the gesture. It had never been this bad before, but then again, she was my fiancé. Not just some girl.

"Almost there," I whispered down at her when we were about halfway there. The walk to the entrance of the building had never felt this long before. Thankfully, though, a minute later we passed the last of the cameras and walked into the building. The moment the flashing went away, Jenna sighed and leaned against me. I smiled softly down at her, liking the feeling of her pressed against me.

"You did good, Jenna," I said, grinning. She grinned back at me, and my heart thudded. Her smile never failed to make me feel better or make my heart beat faster. I squeezed her hand reassuringly as we made our way into the room. I felt everyone's gaze on us and had to hold back a glare. They needed to mind their own damn business. Looking over at Jenna, I felt a sense of pride as she walked beside me with her head held high. *That's my girl.*

As we walked around, I noticed Jenna was wondering what it was all for. After explaining to her it was for a good cause, we continued on our way. Occasionally I nodded at a few men as we walked around. I did notice a lot of them were staring at Jenna, and it made me want to clench her to my side, letting them know she was mine.

"Liam Stanford! It is great to see you again," a

familiar, booming voice said. Looking over toward the sound, I let myself smile as I saw an old family friend.

"Kenneth, it is nice to see you as well," I said once we came to a stop in front of him. I shook his hand. Kenneth was literally like a walking Santa. He was nice, loud, and could be called jolly. He was one of the nicest people I had ever met here at these parties.

"And this must be your fiancé. Hello, love, I am Kenneth Poltz," he said, turning to Jenna. She returned his greeting kindly.

"Wow, she is a pretty little thing. Good catch, boy." Kenneth smacked my shoulder roughly. I swallowed a grunt. That man might be kind of big, but he could hit hard. "Honey, come meet Liam's fiancé," he shot over his shoulder. Moving to the side, he revealed his beautiful, tall wife, Maria. Maria was practically the only wife here who was not stuck up and looked at everyone like they were gum stuck to the bottom of her shoe.

"Kenneth owns one of the biggest stores in America," I said to Jenna, although I knew she probably already knew that.

"That is impressive," she said, smiling at both Kenneth and Maria. Before they could say anything, I heard my name being called from my right.

"I'm sorry, but my fiancé and I better go and see some other people. We will be back to talk, Kenneth and Maria," I said regretfully. If I had a choice, I would rather stay here with them than go and greet others.

"Don't worry, boy, we aren't going anywhere.

We want to learn more about your lovely girl." Kenneth grinned at Jenna, which made his wife roll her eyes. I chuckled, knowing he meant nothing by it.

For the next hour or so, I tugged Jenna along beside me as we went from group to group, saying hello to everyone. Since I was going to take over the company, it was my duty to make sure to say hello to everyone and ask how their families were. It was very tiring and boring, honestly. I had to hold back a proud grin as Jenna talked back to one of a beneficiary's wife after she made it known she didn't like Jenna. When Jenna wanted to be, she could be a little fire-cracker. That was something I was starting to love about her. As we walked toward another group, I felt a soft tug on my hand followed by the sound of Jenna's voice.

"Um, Liam."

"Yes?" I immediately stopped, thinking something was wrong. "Is something wrong?" Her smile calmed me down instantly.

"No, I was just wondering if I could get a drink."

"Of course. No alcohol."

"Wait, how did you know I don't like alcohol?" she asked. I could hear the confusion clear in her voice. When I watched her in the beginning and at dinner at my parents' house, I saw that she did not like alcohol.

"I saw your face at my parents' when we had wine, and whenever we eat you only ever have water," I explained. She stood there, shocked. Shaking my head at her, I dropped her hand. "I'll go get you a water. Just stay right here." After making sure she would stay, I hurried over to the bar. I did not want to leave Jenna by herself longer than necessary. One of the men or even women would pounce on her like a panther. If she was by my side, I didn't have to worry about her. The realization that I could have taken her to the bar with me didn't occur to me until I reached it.

After quickly ordering a water for both of us, I waited impatiently for the guy behind the counter to give the drinks to me. He was taking his fucking sweet time, and when he finally did hand the drinks over, I ripped them from his hand and went back to Jenna. The moment I spotted her, I knew something was wrong. She was just standing there, staring off in space. Her face looked like someone had killed her puppy and they were making her watch. Handing the new drinks to a waiter walking around with an empty tray, I quickly walked toward her. I called her name softly, but she didn't respond. Putting my hands on her shoulders, I shook her gently.

"Jenna," I called softly. This time she did respond. Her green eyes looked up at me in a daze, like she wasn't really here. The hurt in her eyes was so deep that even I felt it.

"I…I n-need air," she choked out. Nodding, I grabbed her hand and pulled her toward a balcony exit. When I pushed open the doors, Jenna let go of my hand and raced to the railing. I heard her taking deep breaths as I closed the doors, not wanting anyone else out here.

"Jenna, what's wrong?" I finally asked after a few minutes. Without thinking about it, I wrapped my arms around her waist and pulled her back into me. I saw two tears run down her cheeks. *What the hell happened after I left her?* Did someone try something? Did someone say something? Because if they did, they were going to pay.

"My m-mother is here," she whispered. I tensed. *Her mother?*

"What do you mean, your mother is here?" I asked.

"S-she was right in front of me when you left to get us a drink. She was with a man." Jenna's voice sounded so broken. My own heart broke for her. "How can she be here, Liam? I thought I'd never see her again, and here she is." I could tell she was going to start crying. I needed to get her out of here, back home.

"Jenna," I said, gently turning her by her waist to face me. "Let's get you out of here." I brought my hands up and cupped her cheeks. With the pads of my thumbs, I wiped away the tears coming down her cheeks. She looked sad and hurt. I just wanted to take her into my arms and never let her go.

"What? No, Liam, we can't go. This is your benefit party," she said, looking up at me. Her entire world was crumbling around her, and she was worried about this damn benefit.

"I do not care. They will be fine without me. I don't want you to face that woman," I said fiercely. There was no way I was going to make her stay here any longer. Especially with her mother walking around here.

"But—"

"No, we are leaving," I interrupted her. Giving

her a firm look, I wiped away the mascara that was smearing under her eyes. "Let's go." After she gave me a nod, I grabbed her hand, pulling her after me. The sooner we got out of here, the better. Just as we made it halfway across the room, someone had to stop us. I bit back a groan and smiled, hearing Jenna groan beside me.

"Liam!" a man said. Looking over, I saw Martin Brotherson, the head of Brotherson's Inc. He was not the worst guy in the world, but he could be slimy when he wanted to be.

"Martin," I said. I glanced over at Jenna after I felt her hand tighten in mine.

"It is great to see you. We haven't talked in a while," Martin said. "My wife keeps asking about you as well." He was talking to me as if he couldn't see Jenna right beside me. Wanting to burst his bubble, I interrupted him.

"Martin, this is my fiancé."

"Hello. I guess I better introduce myself. I am Martin Brotherson." He stuck his hand out.

The pressure on my hand increased, and I started to worry more about Jenna. She needed to get out of here.

"Honey…oh, it is Liam Stanford," Martin's wife said as she wrapped an arm around his.

"Karen," I replied. I did not mind her, but then again, I didn't know much about her. A strangled noise reached my ears, and I looked down at Jenna just as her hand tightened painfully in mine once again. She was staring at Karen with a weird expression. Looking between the two, I came to the realization that this was her mother. Karen

Brotherson was Jenna's birth mother!

"I am sorry, but my fiancé and I have to get going. It was nice seeing you again," I bit out, needing to get her away from here. Without waiting for their response, I tugged Jenna with me out the door. The moment we got in the car, she broke down. I brought her close to me and let her cry on my chest, not caring that my shirt was getting wet. Normally the sight of a woman crying put me off, but not with her. I wanted to comfort her and take all her pain away. The entire ride home, she sobbed, and all I could do was rub her back. Once we pulled up to the house, I gently lifted her up into my arms bridal style and carried her inside. Once we reached my room I sat on my bed, holding her tight against me.

"Jenna, baby, it's okay," I said soothingly into her ear. I ran my fingers over her hair and back, trying to comfort her. She slowly started to stop sobbing and was now softly hiccupping against me.

"Let's get you out of your clothes," I whispered and lifted her up. She wrapped her body around me like a bear as I carried her to the bathroom. Setting her gently on the counter, I pulled away from her and to the bath tub. "Do you want to take a bath?" I watched as she started to nod, but then she shook her head. Nodding, I grabbed a clean wash cloth and wetted it. I went back to her and spread her legs before stepping in between them. Being gentle, I started wiping her face clean of makeup. While I cleaned her up, I felt her looking up at me. I ignored her staring and continued cleaning her up until I was finished.

Our gazes suddenly locked, making me stop and stare at her. I wanted to kiss her so badly, but right now was not the time. She didn't need me kissing her when she just met her mother for the first time in fourteen years. Instead of kissing her, I laid my forehead on hers.

"I am sorry about your mother. I did not know she was Martin Brotherson's wife," I murmured softly. I did really feel bad.

"It is okay," she croaked out. "I just...I can't believe she is here. After all this time she was still in New York, making a new life." Her eyes started to tear up again.

"Jenna, look at me." With one finger, I lifted her chin. "I will not let that woman near you, okay? I will make sure she doesn't hurt you again." I stared hard into her eyes. I wanted her to trust me on that.

"I...thank you," she whispered. Without thinking, I softly pressed a kiss to her forehead.

"Let's get you changed." I stepped back and held out my hand for her. I held back a grin as she put her hand in mine without hesitating. "Here, you can put these on." I dropped a pair of boxers and a grey shirt in her hands.

"I can just go to my room," she said.

"No, you are staying in here tonight," I replied, my voice firm. "I won't look." Turning my back to her, I heard her struggling to get the zipper on her dress undone. I turned around and bit back a smile as she let me move around her. When I put my hands on her shoulders, I felt her shiver slightly. Slowly I unzipped her dress, trailing my fingertips along with it. I couldn't resist touching her bare skin. With the dress unzipped, I reached back up and unclasped the necklace. Being so close to her and her almost naked, all I wanted to do was take her back to the bed and have my way with her. I made myself pull away from her with a groan. Once again I turned my back on her so she could get dressed.

"I am done," she said in a soft tone a minute later. Seeing her in my clothes made me happy. And she looked good in them. The shirt was big and hung on her small frame, making it seem like she didn't have the boxers I gave her on. When I grabbed her hand once more, I realized it was starting to become natural. I took her back into my bedroom. I watched her jump on my bed and groan. My bed was definitely comfortable.

"I am going to go change. Just lay down and relax," I said as she lay on my huge bed, which made her look tiny. I headed back to my bathroom to wash my face and quickly change. When I reemerged, I found Jenna deep in thought. I slid into bed, and she shifted to look at me.

"What were you thinking about?" I asked. I let any comments slide, as she was staring at my chest.

"Just about my mother. That's all," she said.

"Don't think about her, Jenna. She doesn't deserve you." I meant every word. Jenna did not deserve what her mother had done to her. She deserved a lot better.

"Thank you, Liam. I am sorry we had to leave the Benefit. And that I cried all over your shirt," she mumbled softly.

"Don't worry about it. The Benefit is fine

without me, and that shirt was old anyways," I said, waving it away and sending her a smile. I watched as her eyelids started to droop and a yawn escaped her lips. "Just go to sleep. I got you," I said, bringing my arms around her and holding her close to my chest. She curled up against me, and I sighed. She fit perfectly against me. Everything about her was perfect.

Long after she fell asleep, I couldn't help but think of the future. Before Jenna, all I wanted was to take over the business and that was it. I did not want a marriage or someone to be tied down with. But now, getting to know her and be around her, I was starting to think differently. I wanted her in my life. Instead of ruining it like I always did, maybe this time I should start to make an effort. With that in mind, I whispered goodnight to Jenna, planting a kiss on top of her head and eventually drifting off to sleep.

Chapter Seven

Karen

That face. That face looked awfully familiar, but I couldn't place a finger on it. The girl with Liam Stanford was very pretty, and I couldn't help but wonder if we had met before. Even after they abruptly left, I stared after them, my eyebrows furrowed. The rest of the night went by rather quickly, and soon my husband and I were back home. I was currently taking off my makeup and getting into a pair of pjs.

"Honey, do you know the girl that was with Liam Stanford?" I asked from the bathroom.

"All I know is that she is his fiancé," Martin shouted back at me. "She never said her name."

Then why did she seem so familiar?

"Why are you wondering?" he asked as I came out of the bathroom and stood beside the bed.

"Oh, nothing. I just think I have seen her before. Maybe we have met her parents or something." I waved it off. I was just tired from the long day.

"I just got off the phone with Ryan, and he said him and Tessa are excited about coming home, and their plane lands at eleven so we have to be there early," he said. My twin babies were off at boarding school. It sucked not seeing them every day, but it was the best school in the country, so I guess it made up for it.

"That's good," I said, rubbing in my lotion before pulling the covers over myself and grabbing my book. We read for the next little bit before turning off our lights and heading to bed.

I lay there, trying to sleep, but for some reason I could not. I tried counting sheep and thinking about everything I needed done this weekend and during the week, but nothing seemed to work. Instead, my mind decided to bring up old memories I had pushed far away.

***

"What is your name?" someone asked. Lifting my head up from the counter, I saw a pair of chocolate-brown eyes and a gorgeous face. The guy sitting in front of me was wearing a nice suit with the tie loosened, and his brown hair was ruffled like he ran his hands through it too many times. He looked vaguely familiar, but I couldn't place him.

"Huh?" I asked, already forgetting what he'd just said. I was too busy staring at his gorgeous face. He had high cheek bones and a nice jaw line.

"What is your name?" he asked once more.

"Oh, I am Karen," I answered.

"Pretty name for a pretty woman," he said,

sending me a smile. I felt myself blush and chided myself. I was twenty-five, for goodness' sake. I shouldn't be blushing at a comment like that.

"Thank you," I said softly.

"I am Martin, Martin Brotherson."

"It is nice to meet you, Martin." Looking down at his hands, I saw he didn't have a drink, and I also noticed he didn't have a ring on. I really didn't expect him to be married, seeing that he couldn't be older than twenty-eight. "Is there anything I can get you? A beer, scotch, whiskey?" I asked.

"I'll take a beer. Whatever you have on draft," he answered. Nodding, I moved behind the counter to get him his drink. I felt him staring at me the entire time, which made my skin get hot.

"Here you go," I said, sliding his beer in front of him.

"If you don't mind me asking, why is a woman like you working at a bar like this?" Martin asked suddenly.

"What is a man like you doing at a bar like this?" I countered.

"Long day at the office. Needed something to relax me," he answered, surprising me. He raised his eyebrows at me, waiting for my answer.

"I have bills I need to pay."

"A woman like you shouldn't have to work for stuff." He took a pull from his beer and looked me straight in the eyes. Something about him seemed to speak to me. He looked like a businessman, and judging by his expensive watch, he had money.

I had been in plenty of relationships before. I mean, I had a daughter for crying out loud. It was no surprise that I was attracted to this unknown man. But it was surprising by how much I was. I'd only met him three minutes ago. His stare burned into my face like he was trying to get inside of my head.

"Tell me more about you," Martin said, interrupting my thoughts. For the next hour the two of us spoke, getting to know one another. The entire time I felt at ease and safe. He did not strike me as a guy who would hurt a woman or demand sex in the bathroom like most men I had encountered at work. Every time I talked he would listen intently, almost like he was hanging off every word. Before I knew it, it was ten at night and my shift was over.

I knew it was terribly wrong, but I never told Martin I had a five-year-old daughter at home. Something inside of me was holding that little piece of information back. I knew men did not like when a woman had a child from another man. I knew if I told him he would run away, and I did not want that. I wanted to keep talking to him. We talked as if we knew each other all our lives. And we had plenty in common. We both lost our parents right after high school, and we both liked the same type of music.

I learned that when his parents passed away he was handed his family's company. While attending college he also worked at the company, and when he turned twenty-one he took over the entire thing. The company was called Brotherson's Inc. and they sold everything from furniture to electronics. He was well known around New York.

When I was told I could leave, I felt my heart

sink. I wanted to stay and talk to Martin longer, but I knew I had to get home to my daughter, Jenna. She was home with a babysitter right now. I gathered my things that I had left behind the bar. As I came around, Martin was standing right there, waiting for me.

"I guess I better get going," I said, hoping my tone didn't give away that I didn't want to.

"I guess I'd better too." Walking side by side, we left the bar and headed to the parking lot. Both of us were quiet as I walked to my beat up car. For some reason I felt extremely sad that I was leaving Martin and would probably never see him again. I felt connected to him in some way. I couldn't explain it.

"Karen." Martin stopped me with a hand on my arm.

"Yeah?"

"I want to see you again, if that is okay." He stared down at me.

"I-I would like that." A grin spread across his face.

"Good. Would you like to go on a date with me tomorrow night?" he asked. I wanted to immediately say yes, but I stopped. Tomorrow was Friday and I had Jenna. I stood there, biting my bottom lip and thinking. Before I even knew it, the word "yes" slipped out.

"Can I have your phone number so I can call you when it's time to pick you up?" Without thinking about it I grabbed his phone and punched my number into it. "It was nice meeting you, Karen. I am glad I came into this bar."

"Me too." I grinned at him.

"I'll text you later." Reaching for my hand, he brought it up to his lips and pressed a kiss to it. I blushed and he smiled before stepping back and walking away. I unlocked my car and slid into the driver's seat. I sat there, grinning from ear to ear. I had a date tomorrow. The first one in five years.

The entire drive home I thought about Martin, a warm feeling making its way into my chest and stomach. Something about him excited me. When I pulled into the parking spot for my apartment I sighed, looking up at my building. It was not the greatest place to live. I was a single mother and worked two jobs just to make ends meet. If it were up to me I would not be living here, but I had nowhere else for Jenna and me to go.

Locking my car behind me, I grudgingly walked to my apartment building and inside. After I graduated high school my life turned upside down. A year after my graduation, my parents were in a car accident and were killed instantly. Ridden with sadness and loneliness, I got caught up in a bad crowd. I partied every night, having sex with random strangers, not really caring about anything. Before, my life was good. I had two loving parents, a big group of amazing friends, college possibilities, but now, nothing. After almost a year of partying, drinking, and sex, I found out I was pregnant. I had only turned twenty a few weeks before. I knew who the father was, some deadbeat twenty-four year old that my "friends" were friends with.

The moment I found out about my pregnancy, it

was a wake up call. I stopped partying and drinking. I found a pretty decent job and a place from whatever was left of my parents' funds. I had told the father, but he wanted nothing to do with me or the baby. At the time I was happy to have a baby, but I was only twenty. I couldn't even take care of myself, let alone a child.

Five years later I was here with a beautiful daughter and a pretty decent life. Not exactly what I wanted, but it was good. I loved my baby girl so much, but times like this I wished I didn't have a kid. I wanted to act like other twenty-five year olds. Go out on dates, have friends, go to clubs. Instead I was stuck working two dead-end jobs, paying bills, taking Jenna to school and back, and staying home every day. I just wished my life were different.

I unlocked the front door and shut it quietly behind me, not wanting to wake up Jenna. Sitting on the couch with the TV on quietly was my babysitter, Mary. The girl was only seventeen. She was very sweet and got along great with Jenna. She only lived a few blocks away, which was perfect if I needed her here suddenly.

"Hi, Ms. Howard," she said, apparently hearing me come in.

"Hi, Mary. How was she tonight?" I asked, putting my keys and purse on the counter.

"Great, as always," Mary said, smiling. She turned off the TV and stood up. "How was work?" At the mention of work, the image of Martin flashed in my head.

"It was good. Speaking of which, I know it is so sudden and you may have plans, but could you also

babysit tomorrow night?" I asked. I hated asking her when she probably already had plans, but I had no other choice.

"No problem. I have no plans anyways. Plus, I love hanging out with Jenna," Mary said.

"Thank you!"

"So, big plans tomorrow night?" She grinned at me. I couldn't help but blush. "Who's the lucky guy?"

"T-there's no lucky guy," I stammered. Mary rolled her eyes at me.

"I'd better go. I have school tomorrow." I nodded and grabbed my purse and took out two twenties.

"Thank you, Mary." I handed the money to her.

"No problem, Ms. Howard. Jenna is a sweetheart." She gathered her things and headed for the door. "Oh and Ms. Howard...remember to use protection," she said before grinning widely and shutting the door behind her. I stood there, staring after her. Shaking my head, I headed down the hall and into the one room. A soft smile spread across my face when I saw my baby sleeping, clenching her favorite teddy bear in her arms. I went over and re-tucked her in, placing a soft kiss to her forehead before heading to the bathroom to quickly shower and change.

Twenty minutes later I emerged from the bathroom, feeling clean. I was dressed in PJs. Sliding into bed, I stared at my daughter as I thought about tomorrow. With a sigh, I drifted off to sleep.

The whole next day all I could think about was

my date with Martin. Never in my life had I been so nervous or excited for a date. Maybe it was because this one felt different; Martin felt different than the other sleaze balls I had dated in the past. After I dropped Jenna off at kindergarten, I drove to my other work, where I was a receptionist at an Instacare. I thankfully didn't have to know anything about medical stuff, and the job was pretty easy. Just check people in and get their insurance information.

My whole shift, my mind was elsewhere. I felt like a teenager all over again. I felt like I had when I went on my very first date back in high school. It was a great feeling. I'd missed it. Not that I didn't like spending all my time with my daughter, this was just a whole different feeling. When my work shift finally ended, I drove to pick Jenna up. Since I promised her ice cream earlier in the morning, that was all she talked about when I picked her up.

When we sat in a booth eating ice cream cones, I stared at my daughter. She looked just like me when I was little. Blonde hair, bright green eyes, and a wide, toothy grin. I was thankful she looked like me instead of her father, not that the father wasn't ugly or anything. It just made me feel better, knowing that she looked like me. She talked about some kids in her class while licking her cone. She got the stuff all over her face, but I smiled at the sight. It was moments like these I loved being a mother, just staring at her and listening to her talking, even though she mispronounced some of the words.

Once we both finished our cones, we got in the car and drove home. It was four in the afternoon, and I had yet to hear from Martin. Just as we walked inside the apartment, my phone buzzed. Feeling giddy with excitement, I opened it up to see a text from him. I grinned and read it.

Martin: Hey, does six o'clock work for you?

Karen: Yeah, it does.

Martin: Okay, I will pick you up around then. What is your address?

I hesitated for a second, not really wanting him to see where I lived, but I pushed aside my embarrassment and sent him my address. With only two hours until he picked me up, I decided it wouldn't hurt to start getting ready now.

"Hey, baby, why don't you watch some TV? I am going to go shower," I said, grabbing the remote and turning it on the Disney channel.

"Yay!" she yelled, running over to the couch and climbing on it. Placing the remote back by the TV, I placed a kiss on her head before heading to the bathroom.

Taking a shower took me longer than I thought it would because I had to shave, and I wanted to make sure my skin was soft and smooth. I stepped out of the shower and put a towel around my body and head before going to my little closet. I didn't have too many fancy outfits. Most of the things I wore were old jeans and t-shirts. Looking in the back of my closet, I saw a few dresses I still had from my partying days. After I had Jenna I lost a ton of weight, and I thought I could probably wear one of them tonight. I grabbed the three dresses I still had and placed them on my bed before starting on blow drying my hair in front of the mirror beside the bed. While I was finishing drying my hair, Jenna walked in.

"Mommy, what are you doing?" she asked, jumping on the bed and looking at me.

"I am doing my hair, baby. Would you like to watch?" She gave me a nod, and I started doing my hair, telling Jenna what I was doing. She seemed fascinated, her eyes wide as she took everything in. Once my hair was curled and framing my face, I grabbed some makeup. I hadn't really worn any in a long time, but I did not want to go out with Martin looking like a zombie.

"Twis one," Jenna said suddenly, grabbing a tub of lipstick from the counter. I took it from her and popped open the lid, showing her the red color.

"This one?" She nodded. Smiling, I put it on before showing her my lips. Once she saw it she nodded, grinning and showing me her two front teeth. "Since you are so great at helping me with my makeup, why don't you help me with an outfit?" I said.

I held them up one at a time and watched Jenna's face. She was definitely my daughter, as she picked out a cute simple strapless black dress. It was longer than the other two, and after trying it on, I knew it was perfect for tonight. It showed enough skin to be sexy, but not too much. With my blonde hair curled to my shoulders and my makeup done, I slid on a pair of heels I hadn't worn in five years.

"*How do I look, baby?*" *I asked, twirling around.*

"*Mommy, you wook pwetty,*" *Jenna said. Grabbing her, I lifted her into my arms and turned around in a circle. Jenna giggled and smiled as she looked at me. A knock on the door stopped me, and I set Jenna down. I ran a hand down my dress and headed for the door, thinking it was Martin. Hesitantly opening the door, I let out a breath of relief when I saw Mary standing there.*

"*Whoa, Ms. Howard, you look hot!*" *Mary said, looking at me and walking inside.*

"*Thank you.*"

"*Mary!*" *Jenna screamed, running toward her. Laughing, Mary lifted her up and kissed her cheek. Seeing as it was five minutes to six, I grabbed everything I needed and put it in my purse.*

"*I am sorry for making you babysit on a Friday, Mary,*" *I said, reaching for my cell phone.*

"*It is no problem, Ms. Howard.*" *I hated when she called me that. It made me feel so old. But no matter how many times I told her to call me Karen, she wouldn't.* "*You deserve to go on a date and let loose.*" *I smiled at her, and my phone buzzed in my hand. With a text from Martin saying he was here, my heart rate started to pick up. For some reason I didn't want him coming up here and seeing Jenna.*

"*I have to go. I will be back before midnight. Thank you so much, Mary,*" *I said, making sure I had everything. Going over to Jenna, who was in Mary's arms, I leaned down.* "*Be good for Mary, okay, Jenna? I will be home soon. I love you.*" *I gave her a kiss and one last thankful smile I left. As I made my way downstairs, I felt bad for leaving my daughter, but I pushed it away. Mary was right. I needed a night out. I reached the lobby just as Martin was walking in.*

"Karen! I was coming up to get you," he said, clearly surprised to see me down here.

"I, uh, just couldn't wait," I said lamely. Yeah, that totally didn't make me sound desperate. Martin just grinned at me.

"I have the perfect placed picked out." When he held his arm out for me, I grabbed it and let him lead me outside and to a very nice-looking Mercedes. I slid into the passenger's side, and I felt excitement bubbling up in my chest. I knew this was going to be a great night.

The next five months went by quickly. I was happier than I had been in a long time. Martin made me feel so special and safe. We got along great, and we understood one another. After our first date, my life had become happier and less dull. The only bad part about it was that Martin still did not know about Jenna. I couldn't bring myself to tell him on our first date, and now, five months later, I still couldn't. Jenna was still a mystery, and I knew it was wrong, but I liked it that way. I did not want Martin to get scared off by knowing I had a daughter.

I tried to split my time equally between them, but I spent more time with Martin than Jenna. Mary babysat almost every night and on the weekends. She didn't complain since I paid her well for it and she was saving up for college, but I knew I couldn't keep asking her to babysit for me. She was going to graduate high school in a few months, leaving me without a babysitter. Jenna, being a smart five year old, kept asking me where I was going. I just told her it was for work. I felt terrible leaving her most nights, but for once in five years I was feeling free and loved by someone. I did not want to give that up just yet.

We had been together for five months when Martin proposed to me. We both knew it was sudden, but it felt right. We connected in some way neither of us could deny. I loved him, and he loved me. It seemed I was finally getting everything I wanted. I had met the right guy who treated me like a princess. It didn't matter that he had money; I only cared that he loved me. The moment I said, "Yes," I had a huge decision to make. Did I finally tell him about Jenna? Did I call it off? What should I do about my daughter?

The whole next week following the engagement I told Martin I had a few things to do before moving in with him. All week I was stressed out, trying to figure out what to do. I knew I couldn't let Martin get away, and if I told him about Jenna he probably would run for the hills. What twenty-seven year old wanted to adopt a daughter? I could not ask him to be her father, especially after all this time. By the end of the week I had my decision, and I was convinced it was for the best. I settled everything with my apartment, telling the landlord I was leaving by the end of the week. I quit both of my jobs, which Martin fully supported.

Gathering as much strength as I could and

telling myself over and over again that this was the best thing for Jenna, I woke her up early in the morning. Gathering her favorite teddy bear and a jacket, I led her out of the apartment and to the car. The entire ride Jenna kept asking where we were going, but I didn't answer. This was for the best. Jenna deserved a great life, and I was being selfish by keeping her. Or at least that was what I tried to tell myself. I had found a good orphanage the other day. I parked the car a little bit away, and I got Jenna out and walked toward the house.

"Jenna, I need you to stay right here for me, okay?" I said the moment we came to the house.

"Mommy, where are we? Where are you going?" she asked. Her green eyes looked up at me, confused.

"Mommy is just going to go somewhere for a little while, but I will be back," I lied. "Be a good girl and stay here. I have to go." I took a step back, but a little hand wrapping around my wrist stopped me.

"But, Mommy, I want to go with you!" Jenna said, clenching her teddy bear to her chest with one arm. Sliding down onto my knees, I put my hands on her little shoulders and looked into her eyes.

"Honey, I will be back soon. I just need you to stay right here until I get back."

"I don't want to stay here," she whined.

"Jenna. Be a good girl and listen to Mommy," I said, my voice stern. I couldn't stay here much longer, because the sun would be up and the orphanage would be open.

"I want you to know I love you, Jenna. I'll be

back soon," I said, placing a kiss on her forehead. I lingered there a little longer, feeling tears starting to gather in my eyes. I had to let her go. She deserved better than me. Forcing myself back up, I turned and walked away, hearing Jenna crying softly behind me. I had to force my legs to keep walking. If I didn't, I would have turned right around. With every step I took, my heart broke a little more. I thought I was doing what was best, for both of us. Letting one tear slip out of my eye, I got in the car and quickly drove away.

Jenna, I will always love you, and I hope you forgive me one day. *With that, I left Jenna behind and headed to Martin's house.*

***

I jolted awake with tears sliding down my face. I choked back a sob. I hadn't dreamt of that night in so long, but every time I did, my heart broke even more. Fourteen years since I'd left my baby at the doorstep of an orphanage. Over time I had beaten myself up about my stupid decision. I was young and very stupid for thinking I could leave my five-year-old daughter by herself to start a new life. I was so focused on Martin and my so-called "new, fantastic" life that I didn't even think about her. I was a terrible mother.

I had thought about trying to find Jenna over the years, but I figured I shouldn't. I did not want to disrupt her life. She probably had a loving family and was in college somewhere, living her life. I couldn't just find her and say, "Hey, I am your mother. The one who abandoned you all those years ago for my selfish desires." I was now in my forties and had two other children of my own. I loved them so much, and even thinking about leaving them like I did my first made me hate myself all the more. I got pregnant with the twins a year after marrying Martin. It wasn't until I had them and had seen Martin with them did I realize how much I loved being a mother. After giving birth to them, I tried my hardest to be the mother everyone would be proud of. I wanted to be like my own mother, who was amazing and was always there for me.

My life with Martin was great. Fourteen years later, we still loved each other like the moment we met. He still made my stomach erupt with butterflies and my heart race. It really was the life I had always wanted.

But there was still the one big thing I regretted so much. If I could, I would go back in an instant and take Jenna with me. I would always regret what I did and live with it the rest of my life.

Seeing as I was a mess, I quickly got up to wash my face and calm down. I didn't want Martin to see me like this. He could be very protective. After calming down and freshening up, I left the bathroom just as he was getting up.

"Hey, honey," he said in his deep morning voice. Smiling, I went over to him and kissed him. Even to this day there were sparks when we kissed. "You were up early this morning."

"Yeah, I am just happy to be seeing the twins today," I said, half lying. It was true I couldn't wait to see my babies. I hadn't seen them in three weeks.

"How about I go and make you some breakfast before we go get them?" Martin asked, grinning at me. I smiled and kissed him one last time before stepping out of his arms.

"I'll meet you down there." Sending him a wink, I left the bedroom and headed downstairs to the kitchen. I grabbed things from the fridge to get breakfast started, and I heard Martin's footsteps entering the kitchen.

"I am supposed to make you breakfast," he said, setting the newspaper down on the counter.

"You were taking too long."

"Go sit down and read the paper, woman!" he instructed, swatting me on the butt before grabbing my hips and moving me away from the stove. I rolled my eyes and laughed at him, but I did as he said. With the paper in hand, I went to the table and sat down. Martin came over with a cup of coffee, just the way I liked it, before getting started on breakfast. Taking a sip of my coffee, I opened the paper, all of a sudden choking on the hot liquid. On the front page it read:

Liam Stanford and fiancé, Jenna Howard, made their first appearance at his father's company's Benefit last night. His fiancé looked stunning in a simple red dress, and Liam looked handsome, as always, in a black-and-white tux. The pair announced their engagement earlier this week, surprising all of us. No one knows who this Jenna Howard is, but we have to say we are already liking them together. They haven't announced the date of the big day, but we are

118

hoping soon. The two are quickly becoming New York's favorite couple.

Jenna Howard? Jenna? Howard? Jenna? There couldn't be another girl with that same name, right? The girl I met last night was Jenna, my little baby girl?

Chapter Eight

Jenna

"Don't be a baby and come on!" I yelled, bouncing in the air.

"I am not a baby!" he yelled back at me from the doorway.

"You're blocking the entrance. Come on and jump with me!"

"Jenna, you are nineteen and are in a bouncy room for little children," Liam said, crossing his arms across his wide chest.

"So? Does it look like I care?" I kept jumping on the trampoline floor. Getting a few big jumps in, I brought my legs up in a split. "You are just jealous I can do that." My blonde hair flew around my face as my body went up and down.

"I am not jealous." Liam watched me, a ghost of a smile on his lips.

We were currently in the bouncy room at Fiesta Fun, where Lennon and I had taken Sky. It was pretty empty except for a few kids, but they were at the other end. I was trying to get Liam to come in and jump with me, but he was refusing, saying he was too old to be in here.

"Come on, old man!" I taunted him. I smirked as his eyes narrowed at me. "Or do you need my help to get over here, grandpa?" That seemed to do the trick, making him stalk toward me. I would have been scared if the trampoline underneath his feet didn't make him walk weird. Plus, nothing about Liam scared me. I had seen his sweet side often enough to know he wasn't scary. As he got closer, my bounces kept throwing him off balance. I couldn't help but giggle.

"You think this is funny?"

"Well yeah. A six foot three, twenty-four year old bouncing around in a little kiddie place is funny." I stopped bouncing at the look in his eyes. Their light blue color had gone darker, and a smirk was on his face.

"You think that is funny, huh?" He took a step toward me. He was less than a foot away from me now.

"Yes, old man," I said before thinking about it.

"I am going to show you who's an old man," Liam said. I had a second to see his smirk widen before he came at me. With a squeal, I jumped to the side as he lunged for me. "Jenna, come here," he said in a weird, creepy, high-pitched voice. It sounded like something off a horror film.

"No! You have to catch me, Grandpa." I smiled at him. In a split second, he lunged at me again, making me turn and run away. Running toward the other side of the bouncy room, I peeked over my shoulder to see Liam right on my heels. Damn, he got his balance back!

"Jenna, I am coming for you!"

With him right behind me, I yelled and ran and jumped to get away from him. My yells got the attention of the few kids there, and their parents. When we ran past a group of parents talking to one another, they sent both Liam and me looks that said we needed to quiet down. As I kept running away from Liam, I couldn't help but laugh loudly.

I was so busy laughing and trying to dodge around kids that I didn't notice that Liam was right behind me until a large arm wrapped itself around my waist, pulling me back into a hard chest. With a squeal, I lost my footing and slammed back against Liam, knocking him back as well. I yelped as both of us fell back onto the trampoline floor. I heard Liam grunt in my ear as my full weight slammed down on top of him.

"Ouch," I muttered. Realizing I was still on Liam, I tried to roll off, but his heavy arm kept me in place. Suddenly I was being moved and rolled over until my back hit the floor, and Liam hovered over me. I met his blue eyes and gulped as his body hovered over mine, his hands beside my face, holding his weight up.

"I got you," he whispered, his voice husky. I bit down on my bottom lip, feeling a rush of heat go straight to my core and spread through out my entire body.

"You did, old man," I whispered back to him. A grin graced his face at that. His smile was so breathtaking that I knew I wanted to see it more.

"Do I need to show you that I am not an old man? Everything about me is all *young,* missy." He put emphasis on the word "young". My breath hitched at that.

"I need proof," I said, smiling up at him.

"Oh yeah?" His head lowered close to mine. Minty breath fanned across my face. I honestly had no idea how his breath still smelled good when it'd been three hours. His head dipped down lower, almost an inch away from my lips. I continued to stare at his pink lips, wanting to kiss him again. Liam's breath came out in rasps as he stared down at me.

"Hmm-hmmm." A cough came from above us. Groaning under his breath, Liam closed his eyes before reluctantly sliding off of me. When I looked past Liam, I saw a woman standing there with her hands on her hips, tapping her foot. She looked angrily down at us. Liam stood up, holding a hand out for me to take. Slipping mine in his, I also stood and straightened my sweater, my cheeks starting to turn pink.

"There are children here. It would be wonderful if you would not do that here. I think you better leave." She glared at us.

"Whatever," Liam said, surprising me by his response. I expected him to be polite and say sorry. With my hand in his, he tugged me along, leaning down to pick up our shoes by the door. "What a rude woman," he muttered. I bit back a grin, totally agreeing.

"She's just jealous that we were having fun," I said, a smile appearing on my face.

123

"I think you are right." He smiled down at me as we walked hand-in-hand out of Fiesta Fun and toward the car.

"So, where to now?" I asked, reluctantly letting his hand go and opening the car door. I loved the feeling of my hand in his. They fit perfectly together.

"How about somewhere to eat? I'm starving," he offered, starting the car.

"Sounds good to me."

"I have the perfect place in mind." With that, he pulled out of the parking lot and headed to wherever we were going. In a great mood, I turned on the radio. Smiling at the song that came on, I started singing the lyrics for "Somebody That I Used To Know" at the top of my lungs.

"How do you even know this song?" Liam yelled over at me.

"Do I live under a rock?" I rolled my eyes. "Since I am stuck at home every day, I play iTunes."

I kept singing, not caring that my voice sucked. It felt great to just let it out and be myself. Liam kept glancing over at me, but I could tell he was smiling. I loved being the reason he smiled. Turning in my seat, I started singing at him, even making faces along with the song.

"You know, your voice sucks," he commented.

"What?" I put a hand to my chest. "My voice is like an angel's." I didn't take any offense because I knew my voice was nowhere near angelic. I sounded like a whale begging to die while being dragged behind a car.

"Yeah, like a sweet angel," he shot back at me.

"Fine, what's your voice like, oh masterful one?" I asked. "Go ahead." I gestured for him to sing.

"No, I don't sing."

"Come on! You can't say I am terrible if you are no better. I want to hear it, so sing. The song is about to end, so hurry." I sat back in my seat, crossing my arms across my chest and staring at the side of his face. Realizing I was not going to back down, he sighed. Liam sang. I sat there in shock. Of course Liam could sing. *Damn he could sing.* Instead of saying anything, I huffed and slumped down in my seat.

"What?"

"Don't what me! You can sing, you…you butt-bunch."

"So?"

"It just isn't fair! You're good at everything!" I pouted. I was not one of those people who was born with gifts.

"I'm not good at everything," Liam said, stopping the car. Looking out the front window, I saw we were at Rick's Pizzeria. The last time we were here, Liam was being a dick to me, making me leave and get bombarded with paparazzi. "I thought we could finish the meal we were supposed to have," he said. He looked almost nervous.

"Just what I wanted," I said, smiling over at him. Getting out of the car, we made our way inside the restaurant. Once again I was hit the smell of fresh pizza and garlic bread. My stomach made growling noises, which made me put an arm around my stomach to quiet it.

"Liam! Back again?" The same lady as the last time came forward and hugged Liam. "And you brought the same girl back!" She gave me a hug as well, and she seated us in a little corner, giving us some privacy. Sending us a weird smile, she backed away.

"Don't mind Hilda. She likes to embarrass me," Liam said, grabbing a menu.

"I like her," I said, grabbing the other menu. While browsing it, I felt a pair of eyes looking at me. "What?" I asked, afraid there was something on my face.

"Uh, um, nothing," he stuttered before looking down. "What do you want to eat?"

"I don't know. It all sounds so good. I do want garlic bread for sure."

"How about we get a large pizza and garlic knots? They are the best thing to get here."

"Sure." I trusted Liam's choice, since he had been here before and actually eaten their food. After giving our order to Hilda, we sat there staring at one another, almost awkwardly.

"Liam, thank you for today," I said, placing my hands in front of me on the table. "You made me feel a lot better. And I want to also thank you again for taking care of me last night." I was done feeling embarrassed. I had never been that vulnerable in front of someone.

"You're welcome. I am glad I could get your mind off your mother for a while." I hadn't thought of her the entire day, but it was still lingering in the back of my mind, and it wouldn't be leaving any time soon. I just didn't know what to do about it.

Should I try and contact her, telling her who I am? Should I just ignore her? There was just so much to consider, but I didn't want to think about it.

"I also want to say something to you," Liam said, knocking me out of my own thoughts. "I want to apologize for how I acted when I first met you. I acted like a complete jackass to you when I shouldn't have."

"Liam—" I started, but he cut me off.

"No, I was not right doing that to you. I was the one who asked you to do this, and in return I act like a conceited jerk with no consideration for your feelings. I said a lot of terrible things to you that I cannot take back, and I want you to know I am so sorry. If I could go back to when I met you, I wouldn't have acted the way I did. I thought that if I was rude to you, you would take back your decision and leave, but you didn't." He stared down at his hands. "I just…I'm sorry, Jenna." He looked up at me, and his blue eyes shone bright. I could tell he meant every single word.

"I forgive you, Liam." I reached out and put one of my hands on top of his. I did forgive him. I'd forgiven him a week ago, when he started being nice toward me. I knew I shouldn't have forgiven him so easily, but I did. I understood where he was coming from.

"But—"

"No buts. I get why you were acting so rude. Just don't act that way again, please."

"I won't. I promise." Sending me a bright smile, he squeezed my hand.

"Here you lovelies go," Hilda interrupted us,

127

moving our hands to place a big pizza in the middle of the table, followed along with a basket of garlic knots. "Enjoy." When I saw the food, I could feel myself salivating. It all looked so good.

"Since I don't know a lot about you, how about we play twenty questions while we eat?" Liam suggested, dishing a slice of pizza onto both of our plates. It sounded like a good way to get to know Liam better so I agreed. Not caring that I was acting un-lady-like, I bit into my pizza and moaned. I hadn't eaten anything all day, so I stuffed the pizza into my face, completely forgetting Liam was sitting across from me.

"Jenna, slow down. There is plenty more."

"Sworry," I said around a mouthful. He shook his head at me.

"Since your mouth is full, I'll start. Something simple. What is your favorite holiday?" He took a bite of his pizza and waited for my response.

I sat there thinking about it. No one had ever asked me that question, and I didn't have an answer. I hadn't celebrated any holidays since after my mother left me. Holidays were just another thing that I despised. Being alone did that to you.

"I don't have one," I finally answered.

"You don't have a favorite holiday? How?"

"I just have never celebrated any, so I can't really have a favorite." I shrugged. It wasn't that big of a deal. "Anyways, what is your favorite kind of candy?" I switched the subject.

"Nice change of subject." He shook his head at me. "Mine would have to be Snickers. How about you?" Finishing up my piece of pizza, I grabbed another slice.

"Reese's Peanut Butter Cups. Best thing on the planet. What is your favorite sport?" I asked, thinking back to all the trophies I found when I first moved in.

"Football. Fun to play and to watch," he answered immediately.

"Is that why you played it in high school?"

"Yeah, Blake and I were always active when we were younger. To keep us entertained our parents put us into football in elementary, and from then on we played it." I was surprised he actually answered me. When I asked him about it before, he'd just brushed me off.

"So you played three different sports in high school?" I asked. He looked at me, confused. "I found a box filled with trophies and rings from your high school," I confessed.

"Little Miss Snoopy, aren't you?" he teased, obviously not mad that I went through his things.

"Hey, it's your fault for leaving me unattended."

"But, to answer your question, yes I played three sports in school."

"Why did you quit? It looks and sounded like you were great," I asked, wanting to know.

"I got hurt badly in my freshman year of college, and since then I started focusing more on my father's business than anything else." I nodded, feeling bad for him. "You used up three of your questions, so I get to ask that many."

"Fine, go ahead."

"What happened with your mother?" I stared at him, knowing he was going to ask that question sooner or later. He deserved to know what happened when I was younger, especially after seeing me like that last night.

"I was five when she left me. She woke me up in the middle of the night, grabbed a few of my things, and dropped me off in front of an orphanage. Being five, I didn't know what was going on, and it wasn't until two days later I realized she wasn't coming back, even after she promised she would. That morning, an older woman, Sam, found me at the doorstep and took me in. I still do not know why my mother decided to leave me. I used to think it was because she was part of the FBI or something and couldn't come back until she was done with whatever it was, but now I know differently. She left to start a whole new life and didn't bother to take me with her. I was too much baggage, apparently. I lived at the orphanage until I graduated high school at seventeen. Then I emancipated myself before moving out and to my old apartment," I said, summarizing my life story as succinctly as possible. Liam didn't need to know every little thing. He wouldn't care, anyways.

"Jenna, that is—" he started, but I cut him off.

"It's fine, Liam. I don't really want to talk about it. I've moved on, and it is in the past," I said simply. I lifted a hand up and rubbed my chest, hoping to get rid of the ache I was feeling in my heart. It was in the past, but it didn't mean it didn't still hurt. Being rejected by your own mother did something to you that marked you for life. "Tell me about your childhood."

Without so much as a complaint, Liam started

talking about his childhood with Blake and Lennon. I sat there listening to him, and I loved how he smiled at the memories of him and his friends. He talked about all the pranks he and Blake use to pull on his sister, Julie, and Lennon. He also mentioned all his family's holiday traditions and how his parents used to embarrass him in front of his friends and crushes.

As he talked, I didn't feel jealous, surprisingly. Instead, I felt the love he had for his family and friends. He talked about them so fondly, and when he told me about going to work with his father, I knew he had deep respect for his old man. I sat there listening to him talk and silently begging for him to never stop. I could not get enough of his voice, his smile, even his laugh. I took in every detail of Liam from the blue of his eyes to the little scar on the side of his chin I'd never noticed before. I watched as he gestured with his hands about some story, thinking about them wrapped around me.

Everything about Liam I liked. Even his sometimes cold demeanor I liked, as crazy as that sounded. I loved how his eyes shone brighter when he got excited or happy about something and how they turned dark when he was mad or what I think to be turned on. I loved that when he looked at me, I felt butterflies in my stomach, and my heart would start to race. Even when he got on my nerves I still liked him. I loved that he cared enough for me to leave the benefit party last night and cared for me afterwards. I loved that he took me out today to have fun so I wouldn't think of my mother. And even now I loved that he was rambling about his childhood so I wouldn't have to think about my sad past.

I suddenly froze, realizing something. I was starting to fall for Liam. I was starting to fall for the man I wasn't supposed to. I was falling for someone who would never return the same feelings and who only thought of our relationship as a deal, a deal that would end in a year. As Liam sent me a genuine smile, I felt my heart warm up and a smile across my own face. Even though I did not know what being in love felt like, I knew for sure I was starting to fall for my fake fiancé.

Chapter Nine

The weekend flew by, and before I knew it, it was Tuesday, the day I was meeting up with Lilly and Julie for wedding stuff. I was nervous to be alone with the two of them, afraid that I might let something slip. I was also nervous about picking things out for a wedding that was a total hoax. It was nine in the morning, and I had to meet them at eleven at some bridal shop. I wasn't quite sure what Liam's mother had in mind, but I had a feeling Lilly was going to go all out.

I was currently sitting by the window, staring out at the backyard with a cup of coffee in my hand. Liam had left for work a while ago, leaving me to the wolves. Lilly called me yesterday saying Liam was not allowed to come with us today, since we might be picking out a wedding dress.

Ever since our date last Saturday and realizing I was starting to fall for Liam, I felt a little awkward around him. I couldn't look him in the eye. I was afraid he would figure it out and tell me to leave or that he didn't feel the same. I was an open book. I had to get past my little crush on Liam before things started to get even more awkward. We'd been really good these last two weeks, and I didn't want to ruin it.

Deciding I had been staring out the window long enough and that I should go get dressed, I set my feet on the cold tile and headed to put my empty cup in the dishwasher. As I walked to my room, I sighed at how empty the house was. It wasn't bad when Liam was here, because I could talk to him. But being here all alone just made the house feel more empty.

Once I was dressed in a casual pair of black leggings, an oversized cream-colored sweater, and a pair of black boots, I was ready to go. My blonde hair was down, air drying, and curled softly at the ends. I was twirling my ring around my finger, standing in the middle of my room. *Jenna, you can do this. You've met Julie and Lilly before, and you know they are nice. Just be yourself, and it will be fine.* My phone rang. I picked it up and shook my head.

"Hello?"

"Hi," Liam said through the phone.

"Hey, Liam. Is something wrong?" He usually didn't call me.

"Nothing's wrong. I was just calling to tell you my driver will be picking you up here in a minute to meet my mother and sister."

"I thought your driver took you this morning?"

"I decided to take the Audi today. I just wanted to let you know, so if you need anything just ask him or call me. And don't let my mom and sister scare you, okay? They have the tendency to go over the top and make you want to run for the hills." He chuckled.

"Don't worry, I think I can handle them." I smiled.

"I know you can. Just remember you don't have to say or do anything you are not comfortable with. And if they get too personal, just tell them to back off. If they don't, I can tell them to stop."

"Liam, I think I'll be okay. Your mother and sister will be fine. I will let you know when I am back home, okay? I better get going. I don't want to be late," I said, glancing at the clock on my bedside table.

"Okay, have fun. And…I'll, uh, talk to you later."

"Have fun at work. Bye, Liam," I said, hanging up. It was times like these I wondered if Liam really did care or if he was just worried that I would spill the beans on our deal again.

With one last look around my room, making sure I had everything and that I looked okay, I grabbed my bag and headed toward the front door. When I opened the door, I saw the black Cadillac that Liam's driver used. I locked the door and headed for the car. Last week Liam gave me a set of keys to the house, since he now trusted me. As soon as I got close to the car, the driver's side door opened and a middle-aged man stepped out. He looked about medium height with light brown hair, and he appeared to be in his forties, "Hello, Ms. Howard," he said politely, going to open the back door.

"Hi, uh…" I trailed off. I had forgotten to ask

Liam his driver's name.

"Mathew, Mathew Hedly," he said.

"Hi, Mathew. Thank you for driving me today," I said, sending him a small smile.

"It's no problem, Ms. Howard." He smiled down at me.

"Please call me Jenna." I climbed into the back seat, and he shut the door behind me. I sat there silently as he got back in the car and started driving away from the house. It was weird sitting in the back of a car as someone drove. I wasn't used to being chauffeured around.

"So, uh, Mathew, where are we going first?" I asked, breaking the silence.

"Mrs. Stanford and Ms. Julie are waiting at the Highland Town Center for you," was all he said. As we drove in silence, I took out my phone and texted both Sophie and Candy. I hadn't seen Sophie in a while and wanted to hang out with her soon. I was hoping I could hang out with both of them. Who knew? Maybe they could become friends.

The ride continued for twenty minutes or so before we finally came to a parking spot. Glancing out the window, I saw both Lilly and Julie step out of a store and come toward the car. Without waiting for Mathew to come around, I opened the door and stepped out.

"Jenna!" Lilly said as soon as she was in front of me and tugged me into a hug. "It is great to see you again." Standing to her side was Julie. I sent her a smile, and she smiled back.

"Thank you, Mathew. If we need you again, I'll give you a call. I think we will just stay around here," Lilly said, giving Mathew a smile and a wave before grabbing my arm and leading me away.

"How are you, Jenna?" Lilly asked as she led us somewhere.

"I am good. How are you?" I asked politely.

"I'm great! I am so excited to get the wedding plans started. We have so much to do, and today we will make a good dent in that mountain." Julie walked next to me, and I heard her give a small groan. I grinned and looked over at her. She rolled her eyes behind her mother's back.

"I was thinking first we could go to Max's to figure out a color theme, then the florist for flowers, and after that, wedding dress shopping. Then we can get a quick bit to eat before going shopping for party favors," Lilly rattled off.

Oh God, what have I gotten myself into?

***

"I think these lilies would go great with the peach-and-white color theme," Lilly said, picking up a few yellow-and-peach-colored lilies. They were really pretty and had to be my favorite flowers in this shop.

We had spent two hours going over every single color you could ever think of for the theme. Lilly had so many suggestions and ideas that she kept switching colors every few minutes. She didn't slow down until Julie stopped her mom to tell her it was my wedding and that I should choose. Of course, me being me, I couldn't decide. After a lot of talking, we picked peach and white for the theme.

Now we were looking at flowers. I was more than ready to be done, but it seemed Lilly had only just gotten started.

"If we slipped out, think she would notice?" Julie whispered next to me. I bit back a grin.

"Not sure, but she probably wouldn't notice for at least twenty minutes," I whispered back.

"I'm starving. I say we slip out the door and make a run for it." She turned to me. Her blue eyes were similar to Liam's. They shone.

"I don't know. What if she gets mad?"

"My mom, mad? I've only seen her mad a few times, and that was at Liam and Blake. Jenna, I beg you," she pleaded. With my stomach growling, I took one last look at Lilly, who was still blabbing on about flowers to the poor worker girl.

"Okay, let's hurry." Both of us slowly backed away, keeping our focus on her mother just in case she turned around. As soon as we were a few feet from the door, Julie hissed, "Now!" and we both turned, running to the already open door and out onto the sidewalk.

"I think we are far enough away," Julie said a few minutes later, coming to a stop. I stopped next to her, breathing kind of heavily. I wasn't used to such exercise. Looking down, I saw Julie had heels on. When I glanced back at her, I raised an eyebrow.

"How did you run in those heels?" I blurted out.

"Being a model, you have to learn how to. Between shoots and dress changes at shows, you learn to run in six-inch heels." She shrugged as we started walking again.

"Did you always want to be a model?" I asked, actually interested.

"Not really. I mean, growing up I was always told I would make a great model with my long legs and my skinny body. It seemed only logical that I became one."

"What else did you want to do?"

"I wanted to be a nurse, a pediatric nurse actually. I've always loved children, and I wanted to help them in any way possible. But when my a friend of my mom's needed a substitute model for a show, I was pushed to do it, and I've been doing it ever since; I started when I turned eighteen. I love the people I work with and the opportunities I get. If it wasn't for modeling, I wouldn't be the model for Calvin Klein, one of the best companies out there. I've traveled to amazing places for photo shoots and shows. I just…" She trailed off. "No one knows this, and you can't tell anyone, okay?" she said suddenly.

"I won't, I promise." I looked over at her. She was biting her bottom lip, like she was second-guessing telling me.

"I have been taking classes at NYU for nursing for a while now, and just the other day I got an offer to start an internship at a hospital," Julie finally said quietly.

"Julie, that is great! You are a few steps closer to doing what you want to do." I hadn't known she wanted to be a nurse, but I thought that aspiration was incredible.

"But, Jenna, I don't think I can do it."

"Why not? This is a great opportunity, and you

can't pass it up. Why haven't you told anyone?" I asked.

"Because modeling is the only thing I have ever done. To my parents and everyone else, I am the 'model' in the family. Someone with my name shouldn't be a nurse. They should be doing something to make a difference," she said.

"Being a pediatric nurse is making a difference. You are helping little kids and teens get better. Nurses are even more important than doctors."

"I'm just worried about what my parents will say or what Liam might think." Her voice sounded small and quiet.

"Julie, they are your family. They deserve to know and will understand your decision. And you know what? If your parents or Liam don't understand, I will make sure they do, okay? If this is what is going to make you happy, then do it. You are only twenty-three and deserve to do something you truly want," I said, stopping and putting a hand on her shoulder. Surprising me, she leaned down and hugged me.

"Thank you, Jenna." I awkwardly patted her back.

"No problem." She pulled away from me and smiled.

"Now, on a less serious note, let's go get something to eat. I'm starving!" Smiling, I nodded and walked alongside her.

***

"There you two are!" a familiar female voice

140

yelled.

"Damn it," Julie muttered, coming to a stop and turning around.

For the last hour and a half, we had been able to hide from Lilly. We got a quick bite to eat at Panera Bread, and we were even able to go to Victoria's Secret before Lilly found us. I'd never been inside one before, but with Julie being a Victoria's Angel, we were immediately welcomed in and given free reign of everything. Let's just say it was embarrassing having your fiancé's sister picking out lingerie, as well as bras and panties. I had at least three bags full of stuff, and I was going to make sure to hide the lingerie deep in my closet.

"Where did the two of you run off to?" Lilly's loud voice was coming closer. The few people around us turned to look at her weirdly, but she paid them no attention. "I was worried that you were kidnapped or something!" She came to a stop in front of us, her eyes narrowed.

"Sorry, Mom, I was hungry, as was Jenna, so we left," Julie interjected, thankfully. I didn't want to answer.

"You could have at least told me you were leaving!" She pointed a finger at us.

"Sorry, but did you at least pick out some flowers?" Julie changed the subject.

"I did. I put them on hold so we can go back there with Liam. You two can pick out which ones you like the best," Lilly replied.

"Oh, uh, thank you," I said.

"Since I found you two, should we go dress shopping now?" Lilly asked.

"You're not hungry?" Julie asked.

"When I couldn't find you, I ate by myself." Lilly waved it off. "Let's go wedding dress shopping. The owner of the boutique is waiting for us," was all she said before turning and walking off, clearly expecting us to follow.

***

Liam

"Mr. Stanford, your meeting is at three-thirty, which is in five minutes," my assistant said, walking into my office.

"Thank you, Willa," I said, finishing up a text I was sending to Blake. I had gotten off the phone with Jenna just a few minutes ago, and I couldn't help but worry for her today. My mother could be a lot to handle, especially when it came to planning a wedding. Julie would be fine, but if she wanted answers from someone, she would get them.

I'd felt weird ever since my date with Jenna on Saturday. I couldn't put my finger on why, but I just did. I had a great time playing laser tag with her, and then, when we were in the bouncy house, all I had wanted to do was kiss her. She looked so cute, jumping around with her blonde hair flying around her face. She looked happy, and I was glad I could get her mind off her mother. I wanted to see her smile and hear her laugh all day every day.

After hearing the story behind her mother leaving her, all I wanted to do was march right up to Karen Brotherson and demand to know why she would do such a thing. How could anyone leave Jenna? Shaking my head, I forced myself to not think about that anymore. It was starting to drive me crazy.

I gathered my phone and stood, straightening my tie and suit before leaving my office and heading to the conference room. Because I missed half a day last week and didn't answer my phone over the weekend, I was still trying to catch up on all the work. Being CEO was hard, and since I was the son of the founder of the company, I had more work to do because everyone expected me to be just like my father.

I wasn't complaining, though. This was what I wanted. I wanted to run this company as well as my father and to make him proud. I technically was already running the place, but once I married Jenna, my father would officially give me the reins. Of course that didn't mean that he wouldn't pop up and do things around the office or that he wouldn't know every single thing that happened around here.

Ever since I got hurt playing football in college, the dream of being a professional player flew out the window, and I focused on taking over the company. Seeing my father be successful in building a company from the bottom up and still be a great father really made me want to do him justice by taking over his responsibilities. It had been five years since my so-called "dream" of being a professional football player, and now I could not help but laugh at that ludicrous idea. I couldn't see myself doing anything other than running this business. In my football days, I had been young and stuck on an idea, not really thinking of the future.

As I sat there listening to the department heads talking about our hotels and companies, I tried to keep my mind off of Jenna. Since the day I met her, she hadn't left my mind. She had always been on the back burner, but now she was front and center. I did really feel bad for behaving like such an ass when I first met her, and I couldn't have been happier when she told me she forgave me. For some reason I didn't want Jenna mad at me. At first the idea of living with an unknown girl was something I didn't want. That was why I put Jenna in the guest room, which was the furthest from my room. But now, after living with her, I had found myself liking our situation. I liked that she knew how to cook and that we cooked together every night. I liked that she didn't mind staying home at night and on the weekends instead of going out and spending money or partying.

I didn't hear a word that was said throughout the meeting, and when I came to, everyone was starting to get up, gathering their things.

"Good job, everyone," I said, standing up and buttoning my jacket and quickly leaving the room. I mentally scolded myself for not listening at the meeting. I really needed to stop thinking about Jenna so much. *You like her more than you want to admit,* said the annoying voice in my head. *Shut up,* I replied, heading back to my office.

Shutting my office door behind me, I went to my desk and sighed. I looked out my window and took in the view. All I really wanted to do right now was go home and be with Jenna. I wanted to hear what her afternoon was like. I even wanted to tell her about mine, which I had never wanted to do in my life. The ping of my phone had me reaching for it. Glancing down, I felt a smile appear on my face and my heart flutter a little when I saw Jenna's name appear. All her text said was that she was home, but it was enough to make me hurry and text back and for my heart rate to speed up.

Maybe I did like Jenna more than I thought.

Chapter Ten

Lennon

Six Years Ago

The day started off just like any other, but thankfully it was Thursday. I had gotten up fifteen minutes late, which was making me rush to get ready for school. I didn't have time to shower, so I quickly threw my brown hair into a messy ponytail before putting on a pair of black skinny jeans and a cute light pink top. With a little bit of makeup on, I slid my flats on and grabbed my bag and phone, booking it out the door. Yelling a quick goodbye to my parents, I jumped in my car and drove to school. I would have caught a ride with Liam and Blake, but they had to go to school early today for football practice.

Pulling into the school parking lot, I quickly made my way inside the building with a few others who were late. Thankfully I didn't need any books for my first class, so I wouldn't be late. I barely made it into my seat when the late bell rang. With an inaudible groan, I got my stuff out as my teacher started talking.

The only reason I could stand coming to school was because I had two great best friends who made it bearable. Thankfully they were in my all but two of my classes. Blake, Liam, and I had been friends since we were in first grade. Back then, I had just moved here with my parents and was being picked on by some of the kids because I was new. But Blake came to my rescue. He made the kids stop instantly. After making sure I was okay, he asked if I wanted to hang out with him and his friend from now on. Now we were juniors in high school together, and we were rarely seen apart.

Heading to my locker, I grinned when I saw someone familiar leaning against it. He was dressed in his usual low ride jeans and a t-shirt that hugged his frame. For only being seventeen, he was pretty muscular. He towered among the students. It was really because of football that he was in great shape. His blonde hair was wet from a shower he must have taken after practice this morning, and he had on a friendly smile.

"Art thou Blake William, waiting at my locker for me?" I asked, dramatically coming to a stop in front of him.

"Why, yes I am. You should feel very flattered," he replied, smiling at me. I ignored the small flutter in my stomach. Going up to him, I shoved his huge body to the side so I could get to my locker.

"Move it, fatty," I muttered, barely making him move.

"Hey, I am not fat! I am all muscle," Blake said, flexing his arm. I rolled my eyes and squeezed past him to twist my locker combo. Pulling out my calculus and my history books, I slammed my locker shut. *"What did that locker ever do to you, Lenn?"*

"It's fine. I think the hard metal will live to see another day. Come on, we are going to be late to class," I said, grabbing his arm and pulling him after me. The whole way down the hall, Blake whined about going to class, even though we both knew math was his best subject.

"Blake, stop whining! You sound like a girl when you do that," I said, taking my seat near the back of the class. The further away from my math teacher, the better. Ms. Patty—great name, right?—hated me for some reason. I didn't know what I had ever done to her, but she tried to catch me doing something every chance she got. I swear she just watched me, and if I blinked I would get a detention. Of course Blake was her star student though, and she was never once rude to him. Stupid bitch. I saw Ms. Patty glaring at me. Almost as if she heard my thoughts, her eyes narrowed even more.

"So, game night tonight?" The sound of Blake's voice made me jerk my head in his direction.

"Yeah of course." Every Thursday night Blake, Liam, and I had a game night or movie night. We couldn't do it on Fridays because they either had a game or late practice, or there were parties going on. Thursday nights had been our tradition since we started middle school.

After the devil Ms. Patty told us about our

148

assignment and let us work, I stared down at my homework, more than a little confused. I glanced around the room and saw practically everyone scribbling the answers down while whispering with their friends.

"Blake?" I hissed, turning in my seat. "I need help." Sighing dramatically, he turned to me but had a faint smile on his face.

"What do you need?"

"I don't get how to do this," I whined. I was terrible at math, and he knew it. It was definitely my most hated subject, along with Ms. Patty. But put me in a home ec class, history, or English, and I soared.

"Okay, here, let me explain it to you." Blake scooted his desk right next to mine and grabbed my calculus book closer toward him. "You have to..." I tried really hard to pay attention to what he was saying, but with his body so close to mine and his cologne tickling my nose, my mind kept straying.

Yes, I had a crush on my best friend, but that was all that it was...a crush. I realized a year ago that I felt something different for Blake than I did Liam. The day I felt something more than friendship for Blake was when we were having a water fight. As usual, it was Liam and Blake against me, but I had the hose so I was technically winning. I had been so focused on Liam that I didn't notice Blake coming behind me until his arms wrapped around my waist, lifting me in the air. My grip on the hose loosened and turned, spraying both of us. Blake lost his footing, and we both fell to the ground, Blake's body taking the brunt of the fall.

I had turned my body so I was facing him, and that was when everything around me stopped. Liam faded into the background. Only Blake and I were in that moment. His blue eyes were shining bright with amusement and excitement. His wet clothes were cold against me, but the heat coming off of his body warmed me up. It wasn't until this moment that I noticed how good-looking Blake was. Yes he was only seventeen, but he looked older. Staring down at him, I felt my heart start to flutter and my stomach clench.

"Get her!" Blake yelled suddenly, jerking me out of my thoughts. Before I could even do anything, I felt a splash of water hit my back, and then I was enveloped in the stuff. After that day my feelings toward Blake changed, and my crush began. Now, a year later, I still liked him, even though I kept telling myself something between us could never happen. As I sat there with him close enough that our arms brushed, my heart was racing a million miles an hour. Seeing as I hadn't heard a single word he had said up until now, I forced myself to look away from him and focus on what he was saying.

By the end of class, I did half the assignment and understood more than I did at the beginning. Blake was good at teaching me in a way I could understand, unlike Ms. Patty.

Thankfully the rest of the morning went by pretty quickly. Lunch had just finished, and I only had one more class left, Home Ec, my favorite. It wasn't your usual food prep class. We learned to sew, make outfits, and other things. I was walking down the hallway wondering where Blake was, since he hadn't been at lunch with me and Liam. When I rounded the corner, I froze immediately, feeling my stomach drop. Leaning against the row of lockers was Blake, but he wasn't alone. He was leaning down, kissing some girl.

My heart sunk, and my eyes started tearing up. I stood there staring as he made out with who I assumed was his girlfriend. From here I could tell she was pretty, probably a cheerleader too. Blake had never really mentioned anything about dating and up until now, and I hadn't thought about him with anyone. It was at that moment that I realized I didn't just like Blake; I loved him. Hanging out with him every day just made my feelings grow rather than letting them fade. Watching as he kissed someone that wasn't me hurt a lot, more than I ever thought it would.

I made myself go to class after that, even though I didn't want to. I didn't pay attention at all, trying to stop my heart from hurting or my eyes from crying. When the bell rang I quickly left, not even bothering to go to my locker. I wanted out of this school as quick as possible. I was the first person out to the parking lot and in my car. I didn't want to run into Blake because I knew he would see something was wrong.

I was surprised I made it home in one piece. The moment I left the school, tears came rolling down my cheeks. Thankfully, when I pulled up, my parents weren't home so I quickly opened the door and ran up to my bedroom. I fell on my bed, letting out the tears I had been holding in. I was a goner! I was in love with my best friend. My best friend who probably never thought of me as anything other than that. Hell, he was dating some random person and hadn't even told us!

Slowly I stopped crying and just sat there on my bed. I knew falling for Blake was a bad idea, but I couldn't help it. I also knew I was going to be hurt at one point, but I hadn't thought it would be so soon. Glancing at my clock, I noticed it had been an hour since school got out. I bet Liam and Blake were on their way here. My eyes felt swollen, and my nose was stuffy from having cried so hard.

Dragging myself to my bathroom, I splashed water on my face, hoping for the swelling in my eyes to go down before they arrived. I didn't want to look like I had been crying. As I stared at myself in my mirror, I sighed. I should have known this was going to happen. It was impossible for Blake to like me. Lennon, you have to get over this stupid crush! Blake is dating someone, and you have to be happy for him. Even though it hurts, you have to push it aside and be happy for your best friend. *The voice in my head was right, and I knew it. I had to push down my feelings for Blake, even if it was hard. He deserved to be happy, and if I couldn't be that person to give him that, then I would just have to accept that. No one could know that I loved Blake, no one.*

***

Present

There is no way he does not like you.

Jenna's words kept fighting their way into my head throughout the entire week. All these years of secretly loving Blake and I wanted to believe that Jenna was right, but I couldn't. Why would Blake just all of a sudden start liking me? I was no different than I was years ago. I mean yes, my hair was longer and I had filled out more, but still. I wanted Jenna to be right, so badly. Even though I had dated plenty of guys, I still couldn't get over him.

Blake had always been in the back of my mind, ever since I found out I liked him back in high school. While I was dating my first real serious boyfriend in college, Blake's face was still in my head as I kissed my boyfriend or hung out with him. Not even once did Blake ever get jealous when I was with a guy, but I sure as hell did when he had girlfriends.

Over time I had gotten good at hiding my true feelings, but when we were alone, like when Liam and Jenna left us at the pizza dinner, I just wanted to grab him and kiss him senseless. But when I sat there listening to him talk about some girl that flirted with him at work the other day, I knew I couldn't. Or when we were waiting to take pictures with Jenna and Liam for their engagement, and Blake came to sit right next to me, our arms touching. I wanted to believe it was because he liked me, but deep down I knew he didn't.

The buzzing of my phone made me look away

from outside. Grabbing it, I smiled, seeing Jenna's name across the screen. I swiped to answer and held my phone to my ear.

"Hey, girl!"

"Hey, Lennon. What are you up to?" Jenna asked.

I looked around my room. "Absolutely nothing. How about you?" Over the last few weeks, Jenna and I had been getting closer. Even though she was younger than me, we got along great. I didn't care that she took the stupid deal Liam proposed, because I could tell she was starting to fall for him. I didn't think she knew it just yet, but I could see the look in her eyes when we talked about him. It was the same look I had when I fell for Blake. The boys had even had that same look in some of their past relationships.

"Same. I was wondering if you wanted to go eat with Liam and me?"

"Sure, I have nothing else to do," I answered. It sounded better than sitting around my apartment by myself.

"Okay, great! Want to meet us at Rick's Pizzeria in about ten minutes?" At the sound of food, my stomach growled.

"Yeah, I'll be there soon. Thanks for inviting me."

"No problem," Jenna replied, her voice sounding a little weird. Shrugging it off, I said goodbye and hung up. I stood up to get ready, still clad in my PJs even though it was one in the afternoon. With nothing to do for the day, I hadn't wanted to get ready.

Seeing as it was only going to be us three, I just threw on a pair of teal skinny jeans and a cute off-the-shoulder grey shirt. I left my brown hair down around my shoulders and only put on a little bit of mascara and lipstick. I didn't feel like doing my face this late in the afternoon. Slipping on a pair of matching grey flats, I grabbed my bag and phone before heading out of my apartment. Rick's Pizzeria was only a six-minute drive from my place.

The ride was over quickly, and before I knew it I was pulling into the small parking lot. Not seeing Liam's car yet, I figured I was the first one. I opened the door to the small place, and a smile slipped on my face. This place was one of my favorites to come to, with its homey and friendly atmosphere. Plus, who didn't like pizza and yummy breadsticks?

Walking in, I smiled at Hilda, who waved at me. The place was pretty empty, leaving plenty of seats open for me to choose from. I picked a booth and sat there awkwardly by myself, waiting for Jenna and Liam. Hearing the little bell ding by the door, I looked away from the window expecting to see both of them, but it was Blake who came into view. He swept the room with a look which came to rest on me. Smiling, he walked over to me.

As he made his way to the table, I looked him up and down. He was wearing what he usually wore, a pair of light blue, low ride jeans that had a few paint stains from work. An also paint-stained white shirt hugged his muscular upper body. His blonde hair was getting a little long and was messed up, probably from his fingers. I saw how good he looked, and my stomach clenched. *Damn, he is hot.*

"Hey, Lenn, what are you doing here by yourself?" he asked, sliding into the seat across from me.

"I'm not here by myself." I stuck my tongue out at him. "I am here waiting for Jenna and Liam. Why are you here?"

"That's weird. I am too. Jenna called me asking if I wanted to come out with them but didn't mention you."

"That is weird. She didn't say you were coming either."

"Wow, I am hurt you don't want me here!" Blake said dramatically, clenching a hand to his chest. I rolled my eyes at him while grabbing my phone. Dialing Jenna's number, I held it to my ear.

"Hey, Lennon," Jenna said, her voice high.

"Where are you guys? And why didn't you tell me Blake was coming too?" I asked. I wasn't mad that Blake was here, but it was just weird that she hadn't mentioned him.

"Oh I am so sorry, Lenn, but we can't make it. Turns out Liam had to go back to work early and I have to babysit Sky. But you stay and have lunch with Blake."

"You all of a sudden can't come? Well isn't that convenient?" I said sarcastically.

"Talk to him, Lennon." With that, Jenna hung up on me. I pulled the phone away from my ear and stared at it. She did this on purpose. She wanted me to be alone with Blake and finally tell him how I felt.

"Looks like it is only us then," I finally said,

setting my phone down on the table.

"I guess it is." Just then, his own phone buzzed. While he looked at it, I was silently cursing Jenna. I couldn't tell him how I felt. It had been too long now, and I didn't feel like being rejected at the moment.

"Want the usual, you two?" Hilda interrupted us as she placed some waters on the table.

"Of course, Hilda." Blake grinned at her. "And maybe some extra breadsticks for your favorite customers." He fluttered his eyelashes at her. I choked back on a laugh as Hilda shook her head and smiled.

"All right, but only for you two." With that, she walked away to put in the order.

"So, how is work?" I asked.

"Eh, same old. But thanks to someone with Liam's company, we are going to start building another hotel soon, over on Staten Island."

"That's great, Blake! Is your dad going to let you take charge of it?"

"Yeah, he is. He was so impressed with the one we did a month ago that he is letting me do this one too." He smiled at me. "How about you? Anything new?"

"Not really. I think in two weeks I have to go to Miami and help do a photo shoot for Victoria's Secret, but at least Julie will be there too."

"Not fair! You get to see girls in bikinis all the time," he whined, like a little kid.

"Yeah, I am so lucky," I replied sarcastically. There was a lull in conversation as we both stared at each other.

"So, Lenn, I need to tell you something," Blake started, his tone getting serious. Concerned, I leaned forward and rested my hands on the table.

"Is everything okay?"

"Yeah, everything's fine. I just need to tell you something. It is something I should have said a long time ago…" He took a deep breath, almost like he was giving himself a pep talk in his head. The longer he was quiet, the more concerned I became. I had never seen him so serious or nervous before.

"Blake, what is going on?"

"Liam has told me I've needed to tell you this since forever, but since I haven't had the balls to, I haven't. Now Jenna is telling me to, along with Grayson, but I don't know what to say or how to do it," he ranted, fiddling with his fingers.

"Blake?" I interrupted. A small amount of hope was starting to build inside of me. Maybe, just maybe he would say what I wanted him to.

"Lennon, for years now I have…Blake, you can do this," I heard him mutter to himself. I was trying hard to not jump across the table and make tell me whatever he wanted to say. "Lenn, for years now I have…I have…I really like you!" he finally blurted out. I froze.

"W-what?" I stuttered.

"I-I like you. A lot, actually." I watched as his cheeks started to turn a little bit red. His blue eyes were staring at me, and he was obviously waiting for me to say something.

"You like me?" I asked in a daze. For seven years I had wanted to hear him say those words. For six years I had been pining after him, and finally he said he liked me.

"I do. I have liked you since high school. I should have said something when I first realized that I liked you, but you were with that dick Adam our senior year. I realized then that you didn't like me like I liked you. And if you still don't feel that way toward me, then I totally get it," he said, ranting again. Blake had liked me since senior year. Six years. Six years of never telling me he liked me. I stared at him in complete shock.

"Lennon, please say something," Blake pleaded with me. What do you say to the guy you had been madly in love with since you were sixteen, who finally told you he likes you back?

"For six years you have liked me? And you never said anything?" I looked at him, still trying to let the new info sink in.

"There wasn't a good time." He rubbed the back of his neck nervously. "You were either dating someone or busy with work. Or same with me. But the entire time I was with other girls, I could only think of you." His eyes pleaded for me to forgive him. *Forgive him for what? I'm not mad that he didn't tell me. I never told him my feelings either. There is no way I could be mad at him.*

"Blake, I'm not mad at you. In fact, I'm happy." A smile was forming on my face.

"You are?" He sounded optimistic.

"Yes, I am. Blake, I haven't been truthful either...I have liked you since we were in high school too." I blushed.

"You have?" I nodded. "You like me back?"

"I do." I sat there staring at him, hoping I didn't

spook him. Suddenly, a grin spread across his face.

"She likes me!" he suddenly shouted to the practically empty room, standing up. "You like me!" Something inside of me snapped, making me jump up as well and stand in front of him. Maybe it was the excitement that was radiating off of him or the feeling coming from since I finally knew that he liked me back.

Before I could even say anything, his muscular arms wrapped around my waist and pulled me up and to his chest. Automatically my arms wrapped themselves around his neck. Our heads came closer, his minty breath fanning my face. His free hand came up grabbing the back of my head, pressing his lips against mine. Mentally I sighed, finally kissing Blake.

His lips were firm against mine, yet soft. My hands moved up into his thick hair and gripped it, kissing him back harder. I was getting what I'd wanted for six years, and I was not going to waste it. Not caring that the few people were watching, I pressed my body against his. After a few minutes we both let go, coming up for air.

"You like me," he said quietly, leaning his forehead against mine.

"You like me too." Grinning at him, I closed my eyes and breathed in his scent.

Blake Williams liked me back!

Chapter Eleven

Jenna

"Be ready to go by noon, okay? I have to run to the office for a few hours. When I get back, we will leave," Liam said, waiting for my answer. He apparently accepted my nod as an answer, as he smiled at me before leaving the house.

Liam and I were going somewhere today, but he wouldn't tell me where. Yesterday he came home and suddenly announced we were leaving tomorrow. Even though I had asked, pleaded, and threatened in order to get information from him, he didn't budge. How I was supposed to pack was beyond me, and I only had three hours to make sure I had everything.

A whole set of suitcases were sitting in my room, waiting for me to fill them, but instead of doing that, I decided to call Lennon. I smiled as I hit dial. Lennon and Blake had finally gotten together, and it was all because of me. Yes I was giddy, so sue me! Now if only I could get Liam to like me back, I'd be over the moon. The phone rang, and I started to think Lennon wasn't going to answer.

"Hello?" Lennon said into the phone. She sounded breathless.

"Uh, hey. Am I interrupting something?" I asked.

"No, you're fine," she said, but I heard what sounded like Blake in the background yell, "Yes!"

"I'll let you go. Have fun with Blake."

"O-okay," she stuttered, and I heard a moan. Immediately I hung up on her. I did not want to hear whatever she and Blake were doing. I'd rather not have that mental image. Groaning, I realized I had to now pack. I wasn't the biggest fan of surprises, especially if I didn't know what to pack.

Opening the suitcases, I went into my closet and started pulling random pieces of clothing. While I forced myself to pack, I thought about the last week. It went by surprisingly fast. One day I was doing wedding shopping with Liam's mom and sister, and the next I was being woken up and told we were leaving for somewhere around noon.

On Monday, after I shopped with Julie and Lilly, we got to know one another better. To think I was nervous was stupid. They were both the sweetest people I had ever met, and they never once made me uncomfortable. When I had to lie about a few things with Liam, I felt terrible. I did not want to see their faces when they learned my relationship with Liam was fake. Especially after the personal information Julie shared with me earlier. They were what I wished for in a family. I wanted a sister like Julie, who loved her family and would even give up her dream to make them happy. And Lilly was the mom I'd never had. Ever since that Monday, she would call me every day to ask what I was doing or my opinions on some wedding stuff. She seemed to actually care about me.

I was slowly starting to become one with Liam's family and friends. Lennon and I were getting close, and I was starting to consider her one of my best friends. I had only hung out with Blake a handful of times, but he seemed very sweet. I knew I shouldn't be getting comfortable in Liam's life, but I couldn't help it. This was everything I had wanted when I was a kid. I wanted a loving family who cared about me, a group of friends who liked to hang out and didn't care if I didn't have a family, and an amazing boyfriend. I mean, Liam wasn't my boyfriend, but I felt like he would be what I would have wanted. I also knew the more comfortable I got the worse it would be when I had to leave, but for now I was not going to think of that.

I hadn't realized until recently how repetitive my life had gotten before the deal with Liam. I would get up early go to the diner and work hours on end, then I would go home with enough time to change outfits to go to the club. There I would work until the early morning before repeating the cycle. It seemed my entire life had been that way, even when I was in my foster home. I'd get up go to school, come home help with the other kids and do homework before trying to sleep, and then started again in the morning.

I guess I couldn't say my life now wasn't repetitive, because it was. I would get up, do stuff around the house for a little while, read, then, when Liam got home, we'd cook, watch TV, and talk about random things, then go to bed, but it didn't feel like it was repetitive. Even though it was boring, I felt like my life had a little more meaning than before. Sure, I mostly stayed in the house, but I never really got fully bored. It wasn't until Liam that my life was just a boring cycle of going nowhere.

As I thought about my life, my thoughts drifted to my mother. If someone had asked me a year ago if I saw my mother again would I be happy, I would have answered yes. But now my answer had changed. Seeing that my own mother didn't even recognize me at the benefit party was the lowest blow and the worst hurt. I mean, I had hoped she would have recognized me even though it had been fourteen years and I had changed, but my own mother hadn't even shown me an ounce of recognition.

I had wished so many times that I would find my mother after all these years and she would welcome me back with open arms. That she would say she had been looking for me all these years but couldn't find me. Or that she had a good reason for leaving me when I was five. I had not once in a million years thought the reason she left me was to marry a rich man. Maybe she did try looking for me, but I would never know. I did not plan on talking or meeting her anytime soon, or ever for that matter. What she did was something that was unforgivable.

As I continued to pack things I thought I might need into my suitcase, I thought back to when I was seven.

It had been two years since my mother left me at the doorstep of the orphanage, and I was in first grade. It was the middle of the year, and I had yet to make a friend. Since I was in a different part of town than I used to live, I had to go to a whole different school. Even though I had been told I would make plenty of friends, I never did. It seemed I was the odd new girl and that I was cursed or something.

I was sitting underneath this big tree the school had that was pretty far away from the playground. No one ever really came over there, so I was free from the annoying kids. I was sitting there minding my own business, eating my plain sandwich by myself, when a group of kids that were in my class came up to me. At first I had thought they were going to be nice and ask me to play with them, but I was sadly mistaken. Somehow one of the kids had heard from their parents that I didn't have a family. They all stood there, staring down at me while making comments that my mom never loved me and that was why she left. Or how I must have been evil and it drove her away.

For a week straight, the kids made fun of me, but when I stopped crying after the third day, they slowly realized they weren't going to get a reaction. The kids stopped but not completely. They told all the other kids things about me that weren't true so they wouldn't come near me. It ruined any chance of me having any friends. If a new kid started coming to school, they got to them in an instant and spread the lies.

All through elementary to high school the same kids messed with me, but I just ignored them. After hearing how my mother didn't love me so many times, I learned how to numb myself to everything they said. I kept telling myself not to believe them and I didn't, or, well, not fully.

There was always a small part of me that said she loved me, but that part was squashed when I'd seen her a week ago. The kids were right. My mother must have not loved me. That was why she left.

Deciding that I was done depressing myself, I shook my head. I looked down at my suitcase and smiled, proud of myself. I had only filled one big suitcase, and all my clothes were folded neatly inside. Not knowing where we were going, I decided to pack for any kind of weather. I had two pairs of jeans, two pairs of shorts, a few long-sleeve shirts, and a few tank tops. I wasn't going to pack the swim suit, but I wound up throwing it on top. It sounded like a lot of clothes, but I didn't want to pack all light clothes and end up cold.

Mentally cursing Liam, I headed to my bathroom to grab some stuff I would need. I had never left the state of New York before. As I packed I was feeling a little nervous but excited. I had always wanted to get out of here and see new places but never had the money to do so. I didn't know what Liam had planned, but I knew I was going to like it, even if it was a surprise.

Zipping up my suitcase and my little one filled

with bathroom stuff, I stepped back. I put my hands on my hips and nodded. I did good; I only needed one suitcase. Why Liam thought I'd need five, I had no idea. Glancing at the clock on my bedside table, I saw I had a little less than two hours until Liam would be here. Seeing as I was still in my pjs and hadn't showered, I figured I'd better get ready.

After showering, I slipped on a pair of sweats and an old Nirvana shirt. If we were driving or flying, I wanted to be comfortable. I was one of those people that traveled in comfortable clothes and the minute they got home they changed into PJs. I didn't get how people could just come home and sit around in their jeans. It had to be uncomfortable. With my wet hair pulled into a careless bun, I left my room, not even caring if I looked homeless.

I had gotten a lot better at navigating the house than when I first moved in. I acted as if it were my own place, not really caring that it was Liam's anymore. He was home more than he been at the beginning but still not enough. Ever since I moved in, it seemed homey and less deserted. Gone was the pre-paid food. Liam had a cleaning lady before, but now I cleaned the house, making it look ten times better than when I first moved in. At first I was amazed by the size of this place, but now I was so used to it I could walk around with my eyes closed.

Making sure dishes were washed and put away and that everything was off, I was ready to go. I was getting more nervous as I waited for Liam to get home. It wasn't that I was entirely nervous about

167

going on a trip; I was more nervous about being alone with Liam. I mean, yes, we were alone together practically every day, but this was different. We were going somewhere together.

Since I discovered my feelings for Liam, they seemed to grow each and every day. Each passing day I found something I liked about him and another reason to fall for him even more. Maybe it was because I'd never been in a real relationship, but my feelings were growing faster than I thought possible. It was like admitting that I was falling for him opened a gate that would no longer close.

The idea of actually liking Liam was crazy. How could I like a guy who was severely rude to me in the beginning of our deal and who came up with the deal in the first place? Seriously, how could I like someone like that? I had no answer for it. My nineteen-year-old self had fallen for a guy a few years older than me. But you know the saying, "The heart wants what the heart wants."

I was so busy inside of my head that I didn't hear Liam come home, until a hand on my shoulder scared the living daylights out of me. Holding back a scream, I jumped and turned around on the couch only to find Liam standing there with a smirk on his face.

"Scared ya?"

"You can't do that!" I said, standing up and clenching a hand to my heart.

"Sorry. I thought you would have heard me," he said, his face ridden with guilt.

"You're okay. Just blanked out there for a minute." My heart was still beating fast but not because I was scared. Liam standing in front of me dressed in a suit and tie was making my knees weak. The man could definitely work a suit.

"Ready to go?" He interrupted my gawking.

"Uh, yeah," I answered, clearing my mind. Being around Liam made my mind think of filthy things that I really should not be thinking about.

"Good. The flight doesn't leave for forty minutes, so let me grab my stuff really quick and we can get going." He started to turn away, but I stopped him.

"Wait, we are flying?"

"Yeah, is that okay?"

"Yeah, totally." I pushed down my nervousness and brushed past him to get my luggage from my room.

I quickly looked around my room to make sure I had everything. Reaching for my suitcase handle, I froze when I saw my ring box. Damn it! I went over to my side table and opened the box, sliding my engagement ring on. You would think by now I'd be used to wearing this and not forgetting to put it on, but nope. Doing another check around my room and bathroom, I nodded. I had everything. I put my small duffle bag around the handle to the suitcase and put my purse on my shoulder and wheeled out of my room. Liam was already coming toward me, empty-handed.

"Where's your stuff?"

"In the car already," he answered, reaching for my bags. *How long was I in my room?* I let him take my things and head to the front door. Checking over everything once more, I too headed to the front door.

"Have everything you need?" Liam asked, leaning against the door frame.

"I think so. Where are we going again?" I asked, hoping he'd answer this time.

"Nope, not telling you just yet." He tapped the tip of my nose with his finger before moving out of the way for me. Huffing in annoyance, I headed to the car, leaving him to lock the house up. How hard was it to say where we were going? *Jenna, we are going to California.* See? Not hard.

"So why can't you tell me where we are going?" I asked as we both got buckled in and Mathew the driver started the car.

"Because it is a surprise," Liam said. I could tell he was starting to get a little annoyed at my constant questions.

"I hate surprises," I muttered, crossing my arms.

"You hate surprises? Does that mean you hate Christmas?" he asked in shock. It wasn't that weird to not like surprises.

"I don't celebrate Christmas, remember?"

"Oh." The mood dropped a little at the mention of me not celebrating every holiday. Because I had no one, I never celebrated any holiday since I was little. The only time I ever really celebrated it was when Carrie, Thomas, and Lea from the home were around. I didn't want to squash their love for Christmas, so we always did something on that day, until they were adopted. I forced the two older boys, Matt and Ryan, to get presents for them for Christmas day. After the three little ones were adopted and I left, I stopped celebrating it. "Well, I am going to get you to like surprises," Liam said, conviction clear in his voice.

"You got yourself a challenge there, Mr. Stanford." My voice sounded weird to me as I said that. I found myself leaning in toward Liam.

"Don't worry, Ms. Howard, I love a challenge. And," Liam leaned closer to me as well, his voice dropping a few octaves lower, "I always win." I shivered as his breath tickled across my skin, the meaning in his words not lost on me. His voice low like that made my toes curl in my flip-flops.

"Well, you have never played with me before," I whispered huskily back at him. I was surprising myself by flirting back. I'd only ever stupidly flirted with a few guys at the club, but that was only to get a good tip. Flirting with Liam was better. His promises didn't sound empty.

"Then I can't wait to play with you." I watched as his blue eyes flashed with his words. A wave of heat flashed over me as my mind filled with those naughty thoughts once again. I hadn't realized how close we had gotten until I barely felt a touch of his soft lips grazing mine. I couldn't stop myself from breathing heavily as I continued to look in his eyes.

"Um excuse me, sir, but we are here," the driver, Mathew, said as all the heat between Liam and me slowly went away. I felt a little pissed at Mathew for ruining our moment. I watched as Liam pursed his lips, but I told him to thank him. Maybe he didn't want to be interrupted either. Sighing, Liam moved away from me and opened the door. I stepped out behind him and looked around and saw we were in front of a huge private plane.

"Woah, is this yours?" I said breathlessly.

"Well technically it is my family's, but they don't use it very often," Liam answered next to me. With a hand on the small of my back, he gently pushed me forward toward the plane as Mathew and another guy came to collect our luggage.

Going slowly up the steps, I made sure not to slip and fall. If I did, I would have taken Liam out with me, and that would be beyond embarrassing. The whole way up I could feel Liam's eyes on my ass, making me blush. *Of course his eyes are on it. It is in his face.* When I made it to the top I inwardly jumped up and down, happy I didn't fall. My internal celebration was cut short as I took in the plane.

The inside was huge! There were multiple sets of seats at the front of the plane and at the back. In between them was a pretty good-sized couch and a few twirly chairs. A bar sat off to the side, and the bathroom looked to be in the back. Moving further inside, I let my fingers run across the leather seats, knowing it probably cost more than I would ever make in a life time.

"Wow," the word left my lips as I did a three-sixty, taking in everything.

"First time in a private plane, I take it," Liam said behind me.

"First time on a plane," I said, forgetting I didn't want him to know that.

"Well, don't worry, we are safe." I barely heard him as I took a seat randomly in one of the chairs. I wanted to moan at how comfortable it was. I wouldn't care about flying as long as I was in this chair.

"Hello, Mr. Stanford," I heard a new voice say. Looking up from my seat, I saw a man wearing a pilot outfit, shaking hands with Liam.

"Hello, Crawford. Thank you for flying us on such short notice," Liam said.

"No problem, sir. We will be taking off in just a few minutes." The man, Crawford, looked over at me and sent me a smile before nodding at Liam and turning to head toward the front of the plane. I watched silently as Liam unloosened his tie and took a seat next to me.

"I like your flying attire," Liam commented. Looking down, I realized I'd forgotten I was dressed in sweats and an old t-shirt and flip-flops.

"Thank you. I bet you are jealous," I said, grinning at him. He leaned in close to me.

"I think they would look better off." Instantly my cheeks turned bright red, which made him laugh. Before I had the chance to say something, the plane started up and the pilot's voice came over the intercom.

"Will everyone put their seatbelts on? We will be taking off in t-minus five minutes. We will land in Barbados in five hours, so get comfortable and I will let you know when you are free to move about the cabin. Thank you."

Barbados? As in the Caribbean? I looked over at Liam, grinning widely. I had always wanted to go to Barbados and sit on those sandy beaches.

"Surprise."

Chapter Twelve

The first two hours of the plane ride were boring. Liam had taken out his laptop and was doing work while I stared out the window. I got kind of scared when we were about to take off, and looking out the window didn't help. I could see the ground moving underneath us as we went faster. I didn't freak out too bad. I just grabbed Liam's hand in a tight grip where my knuckles turned white as the plane lifted up from the ground. Liam didn't seem to mind my hold on his hand, and I didn't loosen it until the pilot said we could walk around. Even then Liam had to pull his hand away to grab his laptop.

Now, three hours into our six-hour flight, I was about halfway done with my new book and bored. I put my book down in my lap, turning to look out the window. We were currently over some state, but from how high we were I could only see land and a little freeway. My excitement about going to Barbados was over now, as the long ride was not even half over yet.

Sighing, I rolled my head in Liam's direction. A

little while ago he moved over to one of the twirling chairs that had a pull-out desk to do some work. Bored of being quiet and sitting alone, I unbuckled my seatbelt and cautiously walked toward him. It felt weird walking when something was moving, like walking on the bus. Plopping down beside him, I looked at him. He looked really cute when he was concentrating. His eyes narrowed a little, and his eyebrows were furrowed.

"Liam, I'm bored," I whined, like a five year old.

"We've only been on here for a little while," he said, glancing up at me for a second before looking back at his laptop.

"We've been on here for three hours," I replied, deadpan.

"Really? Oh, I'm sorry. I was just got caught up in my work." He clicked a few things before shutting his laptop and turning to face me. "Are you excited to be going to Barbados?"

"You didn't pick Barbados on a whim, did you?" I brought my feet up on the couch, tucking them beneath me.

"No, I remembered you said you always wanted to visit there." He shrugged.

"And?" I waited for him to continue. There was something else he wasn't saying.

"And I have a little bit of work to do there so I figured why not bring you along?" he admitted.

"I should be mad that I am the second choice here, but I'm going to Barbados so I can't complain." I grinned at him.

"What would you like to do once we get there? I have a meeting a few hours after we land."

175

"I want to go to the beach, get some great food, explore some places," I said almost dreamily.

"I'll make sure that you do all that you want to do." He smiled at me, making my heart flutter. "So what should we do for the rest of our flight?"

"Do you have any cards or something? Who knew it would be so boring on a private airplane?" I glanced around the cabin.

"I think there's a deck of cards somewhere here." I got more comfortable on the couch as Liam got up and moved around. "Okay, found one."

As Liam sat down, he took off his loosened tie and rolled up the sleeves of his dress shirt. While he took the cards out of the box, I watched the muscles in his forearms flex. Even his forearms were sexy.

"Want to play a card game?" Nodding, I bit my bottom lip as he dealt the cards.

***

"You are cheating!"

"Am not! I am playing by the rules."

"Stand up. I bet you are hiding cards under your cute little ass."

Rolling my eyes, I made a show of standing up and twirling around.

"See? No cards!" I tried to hold back my grin at Liam's darkened expression. We had been playing all kinds of card games for the past hour, everything from 21 to Go Fish. And almost every game I had beaten Liam. Right now we were playing Old Maid, but using a Jack as the old maid card. Liam thought I was cheating, as I was winning once more. He wasn't the most graceful loser.

"You can't stand losing to a girl, can you?" I smirked over at him, holding my cards in front of me. I only had two more left while Liam had at least seven.

"You're still cheating," he mumbled. I shook my head and finished off the rest of my cards. "I need a drink." Liam stood up and headed for the bar.

"Man, you suck at card games." I got up after him, needing some water.

"I don't suck. It sucks. You suck," Liam muttered. Laughing, I leaned my hip against the bar beside him.

"Don't worry, there are a few other games that I haven't beaten you at yet," I said smugly. A second later I found myself caged against the bar with Liam's arms surrounding me. I barely had to tilt my head up to look at him. His face was less than an inch away. Dark blue eyes stared down at me, and his light pink lips were spread in a smirk.

"I think it is time for me to win at something," he whispered at me. Feeling his hard body pressing against mine was making me lose my concentration.

"I, uh, I…" My hands were inching at my side, wanting to run up Liam's muscular arms and shoulders into his hair. I still remembered how soft it felt under my hands when we took our engagement photos and how his lips felt against mine. Everything inside of me wanted to capture his mouth with my own and have him kiss me senseless.

"Can I win at something?" he asked, leaning his head even closer to mine. I felt his lips barely brushing against mine.

"Yes," I breathed. I was breathless, and we hadn't even kissed yet. He stared at me for another second, clearly waiting for me to go back on my word. Not wasting another moment, he closed the distance between our mouths.

His soft lips pressed against mine gently, almost hesitantly. Something inside of me broke, and I found myself pressing harder against Liam. He took the hint, turning the kiss more aggressive. As cliché as it sounded, I felt the kiss all the way down to my toes. My hands finally got what they wanted as they weaved themselves into Liam's brown locks.

The edge of the bar dug into my back, but I ignored it and pressed against Liam. Once again, time seemed to slow as our lips intertwined with one another's. He felt so right against me. It felt like everything I had ever wanted in my life was right here, right now. Liam made me feel whole, instead of mess of pieces.

We both pulled away, panting for breath. Liam rested his forehead against mine, closing his eyes. I kept my eyes open, studying his face. This close, I could make out every little groove on his face. Unconsciously, my hands moved down from his hair until they were cradling his jaw. I felt a slight bit of stubble under my fingers and couldn't help but think Liam would look good with a beard. With the pads of my thumbs I softly rubbed his jaw line, slowly moving to his cheeks then his chin.

It was like my mind was on automatic as my hands moved of their own accord across Liam's face. I wanted to memorize everything about his face and body. I wanted to feel every groove and scar under my fingers. Bringing my hands up, I gently massaged his temples. I was so focused on looking at his face I didn't see he had opened his eyes until he spoke.

"That feels good," he said softly, his voice almost a whisper. I looked back down into his eyes, finding them practically glowing.

"Yeah?" I whispered back.

"I want to kiss you again." He looked down to my lips, which made me unconsciously bite them. With a soft groan from Liam, he claimed my lips once more. A small voice in the back of my mind was telling me I shouldn't be doing this, but I pushed it away. At the moment I didn't care. Hell, I didn't care about anything right now. Everything seemed right when I was kissing Liam, and I did not want that feeling to go away. Not now or in a year.

"Your lips are so soft," Liam said the moment we broke apart. I smiled, closing my eyes and breathing his scent in.

"My legs feel like Jell-O," I said, clenching onto his shoulders. Liam chuckled before his arms let go of the bar and grabbed my waist. With no effort whatsoever, he hoisted me up by my waist as my legs automatically wrapped around his middle. I squeaked in surprise as Liam's hands moved from my waist to cup my butt. He smirked at me, turning and walking back to the couch. Of course in that moment the plane moved a little, making me squeal and tighten my legs around him and my arms around his neck.

"It's okay, princess." I felt him tighten his grip

on me as well as he lowered himself on the couch. I sat on his lap, still wrapped around him like a koala bear. "I can get used to riding in a plane if it's like this," Liam said above me. Letting my grip go, I slapped his shoulder.

"Are you going to let me go now?" I wondered as my hands left his shoulders and rested in my lap. I raised an eyebrow at him as he just smirked at me.

"I don't think so. I like this position." He wiggled his eyebrows at me, his blue eyes twinkling. I scoffed, smacking his chest. At the feel of his hard chest, I wanted to let my hands roam but refrained from doing so. It was Liam's fault for being so hot that I couldn't keep my hands to myself.

"Well, that wasted an hour. Now only a few more to go."

***

Two hours later the pilot finally got on the intercom and announced we would be landing in just a few short minutes. Both Liam and I got back in our seats and put our seat belts on. Taking the gum he offered, I stared out the window and saw nothing but blue sea. I had almost forgotten we were on a plane while Liam and I kept each other busy.

After Liam and I kissed, we decided to play one more card game before calling it quits. We ended up playing War, which lasted almost an entire hour. Seeing that the game wasn't going to end for a while, we decided on a tie. Since I knew that we were about to land, my excitement was starting to come back.

I gripped Liam's hand once more as we landed, and I smiled over at him. I was finally somewhere other than New York. Barbados had always been on my wish list to visit, and I was finally going to do so. All my thoughts about Liam and me kissing were pushed to the back of my mind as the wheels of the plane touched down.

After the kiss, I had gotten off Liam's lap and tried to pretend what happened wasn't a big deal. The main word there was "tried". While Liam acted like nothing had happened, I was internally squealing and jumping up and down. I didn't know what it meant for Liam and me, but at the moment I did not even care.

Once we had landed, I followed after Liam, excitement bubbling up inside of me. Exiting the plane, I came to a stop, my feet touching the pavement. I glanced around, already not believing how pretty it was here. Of course being at the airport runway, I couldn't see much, but I knew the beach was a little bit further away.

When I felt a small touch on my back, I turned to see Liam standing next to me, waiting patiently for me to move toward a car that just pulled up. Nodding silently to him, I walked toward the car with him following me. I smiled in thanks to the driver that opened the door for me, and I slid in the back.

"We have a little bit of a drive to get to our hotel," Liam said as he buckled himself in. I didn't say anything as I turned to the window, wanting to see everything that we passed by.

As we drove toward our hotel, the trees grew less thick, and more people could be seen walking alongside the road. It couldn't have been more than ten minutes later when we came to the middle part of a town. Cute little stores lined the streets, with tourists walking along the sidewalk. People riding bicycles, skateboards, or roller skates dodged walkers. To my right, on Liam's side, I could see the ocean through the palm trees.

Cracking my window, I breathed in the salty fresh air. Although it was nearing six at night, the sun was still pretty high in the sky, signaling it wouldn't be sunset for a few more hours. I practically stuck my head out the window as we passed more stores and big hotels.

A few minutes later, the car started to slow down and turn into a huge hotel. As we pulled up, I could see there were cabanas off to the side, and there were probably more in the back. Knowing the beach was right behind it, I immediately jumped out of the car just as the driver put the car in park. Behind me I could hear Liam chuckling at me, but I didn't care. I knew I wouldn't be able to do a lot today before the sun disappeared, but that wouldn't stop me from being excited.

"Welcome, sir!" a young man said almost nervously as he came up to Liam. "We will grab your bags and have them sent to your room immediately."

"Thank you," was all Liam said before tugging on my arm and leading me away from the car. The air was warm but a little chilly, making me glad I packed a small sweater at the last second. It would be cold tonight.

"Where are you going, Liam? The hotel is that way," I pointed out as he led us away from the main lobby of the hotel.

"I know. We aren't staying there."

"But don't you have to check in? You can't do that to a hotel."

"Jenna, I own the hotel. It's fine," he said. I walked beside him with my mouth open. I didn't know why I didn't know he owned it. I actually should have expected it. "Flies will fly in your mouth if you keep it open like that." I quickly snapped it shut. Not saying a word, I continued with Liam as we walked to the back of the hotel building toward a set of big cabanas that lined the ocean. They still looked like part of the hotel but closer to the water and probably bigger than the rooms in the building.

"We are staying in one of those," I said, more of a statement than a question. The closer we got, the more potent the smell of the ocean became. Not even looking at the "room" we were staying in, I looked out at the ocean. Just a few feet away was white sand that looked so soft. Quite a few people were out lying around or playing in the water, but not as much as I thought there would be. The water was crystal blue and glowed from the sunlight.

We came to a door, which Liam opened, softly shoving me in and blocking my view. I was even more impressed when I stepped into the room. It was huge! Way bigger than it looked on the outside. In front of me was a big living room that was furnished with expensive-looking couches and chairs, along with a TV. To my left was a kitchenette that was the same size as my old apartment's. And then to my right was a hallway that I bet led to the bedroom(s). *Wow. This place is incredible.*

"This can't be a place at a hotel," I said randomly. "It is the size of my old apartment back in New York. I bet this costs more than an actual home," I muttered.

"I usually don't stay in this part, but I thought you would like to." Glancing over at Liam, I saw him standing at the entrance with his hands in his pant pockets. He was watching me closely, waiting for my reaction. Smiling, I made my way toward him and wrapped my arms around his waist, pushing my face into his chest.

"I love it! Thank you." I squeezed him tightly. I felt one arm wrap around my waist and the other came up to hold the back of my neck. It had to be the best hug I had ever received. It made me feel safe and loved, like Liam didn't want me to go.

"Glad you like it." I felt something like a soft kiss on top of my head, but as soon as I felt it Liam retracted his arms. "I sadly have a meeting to go to in about twenty minutes," he said, glancing down at his watch.

"Oh yeah." I tried not to sound disappointed. I wish Liam could just stay here with me, but I knew he had work to do. He was taking over a huge company, and I couldn't expect him to drop all his responsibilities just for me.

"How about I take you out tonight? Like on a

real date. No press, no one who knows who we are. Nothing but us," Liam said, looking at me.

"Are you asking me out, Mr. Stanford?" I asked, teasing.

"I am. A first real date." A small smile graced his lips. Lips that I kissed not even three hours ago.

"I accept."

"Good. Meet me at The Tides inside the hotel at eight. It is on the first floor. If I'm not there before you, tell the front desk who you are," he said, the corner of his mouth tilting into a smirk. I opened my mouth to say something, but a knock on the door interrupted me. Liam opened it, revealing two men carrying our luggage.

"Your luggage, sir." With a nod, Liam stepped aside and let them place them in the entry. Glancing down at my suitcase, I tried to remember what I packed and if any of it was good enough for a date tonight with Liam.

"Let's put these in our room. Then I have to leave." Grabbing my luggage after slapping Liam's hand away, I followed him down the hall. Straight down the hall was the bedroom that Liam went into. I bit my bottom lip, glancing in the other doors only to find the place had only one bedroom.

"Jenna, come put your bag in here," Liam called out.

"There's not another room?"

"No, you are sharing with me," he said. I gulped at the idea of sleeping in the same bed as Liam. After a deep breath, I walked into the room, only to pause seeing Liam's bare back facing me. The muscles in his back flexed as he reached for a shirt.

I sucked my bottom lip into my mouth at the sight, wanting to run my hands down it. *You will soon enough.* Unfortunately the sight of Liam's back disappeared as he slipped on a new dress shirt.

Before I could get caught gawking at him, I went and set my suitcase by the closet, trying to get my bearings. On a romantic island alone with Liam, I had to make sure I had a level head.

"Okay I have to get going. But meet me there at eight, okay? This meeting shouldn't be long," Liam said, making me turn around.

"I'll be there. I'll be the person dressed terribly."

"You can never look terrible." He walked toward me and came to a stop just inches away from me. Leaning down, he laid a soft kiss to my lips. "I'll see you there," he said, pulling away a second later. He sent me a wide smile and turned and left the bedroom. A second later I heard the door close.

I brought a hand to my lips and let a big grin spread across my face. All the feelings I had been holding in from the plane burst free. Squealing, I jumped around the room and did a little dance. Liam finally kissed me! I didn't even have to make him do it. When I settled down a little, I touched my lips again. What was Liam doing to me?

***

After my little squealing fest I hurried and jumped in the shower. I didn't want to look like a hobo on this date with Liam. A real date, our real first date. I didn't know what this meant for us, but I was liking the idea that we might be more than just a business deal. Making sure I was all clean and shaved, I left the bathroom to find an outfit.

When I was going through my suitcase, I noticed I didn't bring anything fancy at all. When packing I hadn't thought about it. Leafing through more clothes, a piece of clothing caught my eye. I pulled it out and slowly nodded. It was a cute, flowy summer dress. It was white with pink and purple birds on it. It had thin white straps and a brown thin belt around the waist. It would have to do.

Once I had the dress on, I went to do my hair. Not wanting to look like I was trying too hard, I quickly blew dry my blonde hair and left it in its slightly wavy state. With a little bit of mascara to make my green eyes pop and a small amount of foundation, I looked in the mirror. I swiped on some pale pink lipstick and smiled at myself. I looked good, actually.

Seeing as I packed only a pair of tall black high heels, I slid them on, hoping they matched. I glanced at my phone and, seeing it was fifteen minutes to eight, I quickly grabbed my bag and my ring and left the room. Not really knowing where I was going, I followed the signs that were on the walls leading to the lobby.

When I finally made it to the lobby, I noticed I was actually overdressed. Families moved around me wearing bathing suits or just casual jean shorts and tank tops. I even saw a few men wearing those ugly bright flower button-up shirts. Typical dad look. As I made my way to the restaurant where I was meeting Liam, I looked around the hotel. It was gorgeous inside. It had a friendly, family feel about it, even though it looked expensive.

"Uh, hi," I said, coming up to the front desk of the restaurant. A girl about my age or maybe a few years older looked up at me, wearing a friendly smile.

"Hello. Are you here to eat?" she asked, reaching for one menu.

"I'm actually here to meet someone. I'm Jenna Howard." I remembered Liam saying to tell them my name.

"Oh! Mr. Stanford said you would be here. Follow me. We have a table set up for you already," the girl said upon hearing my name. Following after her, I saw the place was pretty packed. I thought it would be a very expensive place to eat and that you had to wear fancy clothing, but it was the opposite. People were dressed in all different kinds of attire, and little kids were talking loud. I smiled at a little girl who was staring at me as we passed.

"Here you are, Ms. Howard," the girl said, coming to a stop in front of a booth that was kind of in the back.

"Thank you," I said gratefully.

"Mr. Stanford should be here shortly." With a smile, she left. The booth was sitting in front of a large window that overlooked the ocean. The sun was starting to go down, and I noticed our table would have a great view.

A waiter brought a glass of water for me before leaving. Not wanting to look like a loser, I took out my phone and texted Sophia, Candy, and Lennon. Since I didn't get a reply from any of them for a few minutes, I went through my Facebook.

Ten minutes had passed, and I was still sitting in the booth by myself. The only person to reply to me was Sophia, but she could only text me for a minute because she was at work. Putting my phone on the table, I looked out the window. Any minute the sun would set, bathing the restaurant a pretty color.

After another twenty minutes had passed, I started to get worried. It had been over half an hour since I was supposed to meet Liam here. *Shouldn't he be here by now?* I wondered. I twirled my phone in my hands, pondering if I should text him. His meeting could just be longer than he thought. Deciding I should, I sent Liam a quick text.

Jenna: Hey. Um, I'm at the restaurant. Your meeting probably went long. I'm just getting a little worried. Let me know when you are coming.

I hit "Send," biting my bottom lip. Setting my phone back on the table, I looked out the window that was now dark. The sun had set a little bit away, and it was beautiful. It was a gorgeous pink and orange color.

"Hello, miss, would you like to order something?" The waiter came over to ask for the second time.

"Oh no, I'm okay. He should be here in just a moment." I sent him a smile as he left. My stomach was growling since I hadn't eaten since this morning. But I didn't want to eat without Liam. He should be here any moment.

I watched as many people came and went from

the restaurant. People came, got their meals, and left as I sat in the same seat. It had been now over an hour since our meeting time. I kept checking my phone to make sure I didn't miss a call or text from Liam. The waiter had been over at my table four times, and I was starting to think he was feeling bad for me.

The look he sent me was like he had seen this before. The sinking feeling of Liam standing me up was getting worse. He probably did this all the time with girls. Got them here, then left them waiting for him like a chump. The idea that he was off making out or having sex with someone else popped into my head multiple times. Deciding on waiting another few minutes for him, I drank my third glass of water.

I felt like an idiot still sitting here, waiting for Liam. He said he would be here at eight, and it was nine-fifteen. *His meeting is probably late,* I kept telling myself, but I was starting to not believe it anymore. Sitting there, I felt all the wait staff's pity. I sunk lower in the booth. I had gotten dressed up for nothing. Here I thought Liam would actually come and we could have a date. The stupid hope that he would admit he liked me and that our deal was off was shattered. I was probably just a thing to keep him busy when he didn't have a girl.

My heart sunk as even more time passed. My love for him was the only reason I was staying. I wanted to believe he would show up any minute and apologize that his meeting went long, but I knew I was holding onto a thin line of hope. Feelings tears burning my eyes, I swallowed the lump in my throat. Knowing he wasn't coming, I grabbed my phone and bag before sliding out of the booth.

I grabbed a few dollars from my bag and set them on the table and made my way out of the restaurant. I kept my head down as the same hostess shot me a sad smile. I didn't know which one was worse, the looks of pity or the look that I was just another girl who had fallen for this.

I was angry and hurt as I walked back toward the room. I had actually thought he would show. *Stupid Jenna. I was stupid for even thinking that.* Bringing my hands up, I brushed away the tears that were starting to leak out. When I arrived at our room, I stared at the door. I didn't have a key. I didn't think about looking for one before I left. I thought since I was coming back with Liam, I could get back in.

Dropping my bag with my phone in it at the door, I turned and headed for the beach. Once I hit sand I slipped off my heels and held them, walking barefoot. Images of Liam pressing some random girl against a wall, kissing her, came to mind. One after another the images appeared, almost mocking me for believing that Liam could maybe like me.

Coming to the water's edge, I stared out at the dark ocean, which was lit by the moon. Tears flowed freely down my cheeks, ruining my makeup. Not even the slight chill of the water hitting my toes registered in my head. All the words I have been called—worthless, will always be alone, not loved—echoed in my mind. Just another fantasy of mine, broken.

With shoes in hand, I walked down the

waterline. Sand squished between my toes, and I breathed in deeply. The tears were stopping and drying on my cheeks. The fresh air made me feel a little better.

"Hello," a random voice said, making me jump. "Sorry! I thought you heard me," the same person said. Turning, I saw a guy around Liam's age standing a few feet away from me, his hands out. I put a hand to my chest to stop my heart from racing.

"That's okay," I said, but my voice sounded weird.

"Are you okay?" He took a few steps closer but didn't come too close.

"I'm fine." The moon hit his face and showed that he was handsome. It was still too dark to make out finer details, but I could tell he was shirtless and had a nice body.

"You don't sound like it. Why is a girl like you alone out here?"

"Long story," I said softly.

"Guy trouble, huh?" he commented. He came to a stop beside me.

"That obvious?" I looked at him.

"Even in the dark I can see you are gorgeous, so it's a given you have a boyfriend."

"Or something like that," I mumbled.

"What did he do?" the guy asked as we slowly walked.

"He, uh, he stood me up," I answered, looking down at my feet.

"Wow, stupid guy," he said. I looked up at him. "He must not know what he has." I stared at him, almost waiting for him to hit on me. He must have seen the look on my face, because he smiled. "Don't worry, I won't come onto you. I don't swing that way." He winked at me.

"Ohhh." Noticing we had gone a long way, I turned and the guy followed me.

"I'm Devon, by the way," he introduced himself.

"I'm Jenna."

"If I can say, your boyfriend shouldn't have stood you up," Devon said.

"I would like to think he didn't mean to, but I don't know." I kicked the sand.

"You really like him," he replied.

"How can you tell?" I muttered sarcastically.

"You wouldn't be out here by yourself if you didn't. If you didn't like him you would have gotten drunk and done something stupid, but no, you are here."

"You've done that, I take it."

"Plenty of times. Being gay isn't the easiest, but I've found my perfect guy." I saw him smile.

"Is he not here?" I asked, looking around and spotting a group of people ahead.

"He's over there." He gestured to the group. "I saw you walking alone and thought I'd keep you company."

"Well thank you, Devon," I said, smiling softly.

"If I may ask, does the guy know you like him this much?"

"No, he doesn't."

"Why haven't you told him?" Devon asked.

"Because I know what he'll say. He probably won't feel the same," I said sadly. Liam could never like me.

"How do you know? Sometimes you have to go for it even if you get your heart broken in the process. If you don't tell him, and he does feel the same, you will regret it forever."

"For a stranger I just met, you are pretty smart," I said, laughing softly.

"I've got experience." He smiled at me. "You have to decide if he is worth fighting for. Even though he stood up, do you still like him enough to forgive him and tell him your feelings?"

"I—" I started, but the sound of my name being yelled stopped me. Looking away from Devon, I saw a tall figure stalking toward me.

"Jenna!" I heard a familiar voice yell again, and I recognized it. Liam. He came to a stop in front of us a second later. His blue eyes seemed to glow in the dark as he looked from me to Devon. "Who the hell is this?" he asked, his voice low, almost dangerous.

"Liam," I breathed, staring at him. *He came after you.* "Who the hell are you? Why are you with my fiancé?" Liam boomed, taking a step closer to Devon.

"I'm making sure your 'fiancé' is okay," Devon said plainly. Seeing Liam's eyes flash, I jerked out of my trance.

"Liam, stop!" I said, taking a step toward him.

"She is mine. Don't you go near her," he threatened, coming closer to Devon. Devon shot me a look, silently asking if this was the guy. I gave him a slight nod before looking back at Liam.

"If she is yours, then why did you stand her up, hm?" Devon had to go and say. I mentally smacked my forehead. I shot Devon a look. I'd never seen

Liam this angry or scary before.

"I did not stand her up. Now step away from my girl!" His blue eyes narrowed.

"Liam, stop. Devon, you better go," I said and stepped between them, putting a hand on Liam's chest. I didn't want him to hit Devon.

"Will you be okay alone?" Devon asked, glancing at me before going back to Liam.

"Yeah, I'll be fine. Thank you for the advice, Devon. I hope I see you again." I gave him a smile.

"He likes you," was all Devon said before sending me a smile and heading back to his group.

"What are you doing out here, especially with another man?" Liam said the moment Devon was out of earshot.

"I was not with another man. Devon was just talking to me, Liam."

"He was looking at you like he wanted to take your clothes off!" he growled down at me.

"At least that's someone," I said before thinking.

"What is that supposed to mean? I am the only person who can take your clothes off, Jenna."

"It means you left me, Liam!" I finally blew up. "I sat in that restaurant like a chump for almost two hours, waiting for you! You didn't answer my texts either!" I yelled.

"I had to sit there while all the waiters kept asking me if I wanted to order and giving me pity looks! You said you would be there at eight, Liam, and you weren't. You made me feel so stupid sitting there waiting for you." I pushed past him, heading toward the room.

"Jenna," Liam said, grabbing my arm and

pulling me back.

"No, Liam! I thought tonight would be different! I thought that since we kissed, we could finally be something. I thought that maybe you liked me too. I am so fucking stupid for liking you!" I couldn't stop myself from punching his chest. I was crying once more.

"Everything you do makes me like you more. And kissing me didn't help! I bet you don't even care what I feel because you have tons of girls hanging off your arm. I bet you were off sleeping with one while I waited for you. Well, you know what, Liam?" I looked at him, hurt and beyond angry. "I'm done! I can't be a part of this deal anymore! I can't lie to your wonderful family. I can't keep liking you in secret while you go off sleeping with other women." I shook my head. "I'm just done," I said softly. Pulling my arm from Liam's grip, I turned and started walking away.

"Jenna, you can't do this!" Liam yelled. I heard his breathing, and the next thing I knew I was being whirled around and slammed against a hard chest. "You can't say those kinds of things and just walk away. You can't walk away from me! You are mine." With that, he slammed his lips hard against mine. I sunk against him, kissing him back just as hard. I put all of my emotions into it and gripped onto Liam's forearms as he cupped my face.

His tongue slipped past my lips and battled against mine. The kiss was hard and aggressive. My body was pressed against his, but I pressed even more, wanting to be as close to him as possible. I bit his bottom lip and grinned internally at the sound of his low groan. Liam's hands left my face and went into my hair, tugging on it to bring my mouth somehow closer. We broke apart a minute later, gasping for air.

"Jenna, I like you. No, I don't like you. I. Love. You," Liam said breathlessly, staring down at me.

"You love me?" I questioned, my lips tingling and feeling tender.

"Yes, you idiotic woman. I love you." My heart wanted to burst at the seams. Liam Stanford loved me! Little old Jenna! I stared into his blue eyes, almost not believing him. "You have to say something," he said as I kept staring at him. Without warning, I stood up on my toes and grabbed his head and kissing him. A soft breeze surrounded us, making me shiver, but I didn't care if I was cold. The heat from Liam's body was warming me up as I pressed against him. Pulling away, I leaned my forehead against his.

"I love you too, you doofus."

Acknowledgements

I want to thank everyone once again for helping me with this journey.

Thank you to my parents, who support me in wanting to write. Thank you to my friend, Arianna, for pushing me to continue on writing and letting me know if my stuff sucks or not. And thank you to all the friends I have made on Wattpad. You guys keep pushing me to come up with new stories for people to read. I love your encouraging words, and without you guys I literally wouldn't have even thought it would be possible to write and now get published. Thank you!

About the Author

Currently lives in a small town called Mesquite, Nevada. She is going to college to be an English teacher and writes on the side. When she isn't busy with school work or writing new books she likes to hang out with her family, do things outdoors, and read whatever she can get her hands on.

Facebook:
https://www.facebook.com/kenadee.bryant

Twitter:
https://twitter.com/kendoll350

Goodreads:
https://www.wattpad.com/user/OutOfMyLimit17